Cassiar's Elusive Gold

Francis E. Caldwell

First printing February 2000
Cover design: Nancy Smith

Printed in Canada

Canadian Cataloguing in Publication Data

Caldwell, Francis E.
  Cassiar's elusive gold

  ISBN 1-55212-337-5

  I. Title.
PS3553.A39494C37 2000   813'.6   C00-910245-0

TRAFFORD

This book was published on-demand in cooperation with Trafford Publishing.
On-demand publishing is a unique process and service of making a book available for retail sale to the public taking advantage of on-demand manufacturing and Internet marketing.
On-demand publishing includes promotions, retail sales, manufacturing, order fulfilment, accounting and collecting royalties on behalf of the author.

Suite 6E, 2333 Government St., Victoria, B.C. V8T 4Z1, CANADA
Phone   250-383-6864   Toll-free 1-888-232-4444 (Canada & US)
Fax   250-383-6804   E-mail   sales@trafford.com
Web site www.trafford.com trafford publishing is a division of trafford holdings ltd.
Trafford Catalogue #00-0001   www.trafford.com/robots/00-0001.html

10   9   8   7   6   5   4   3   2

Dedication

This book is dedicated to the countless thousands of stampeders who gave their all to finding the elusive yellow metal, under unimaginable primitive conditions, then were forced to admit defeat. Remember the words of Robert Service: "Yet it isn't the gold that I'm wanting, So much as just finding the gold."

CONTENTS

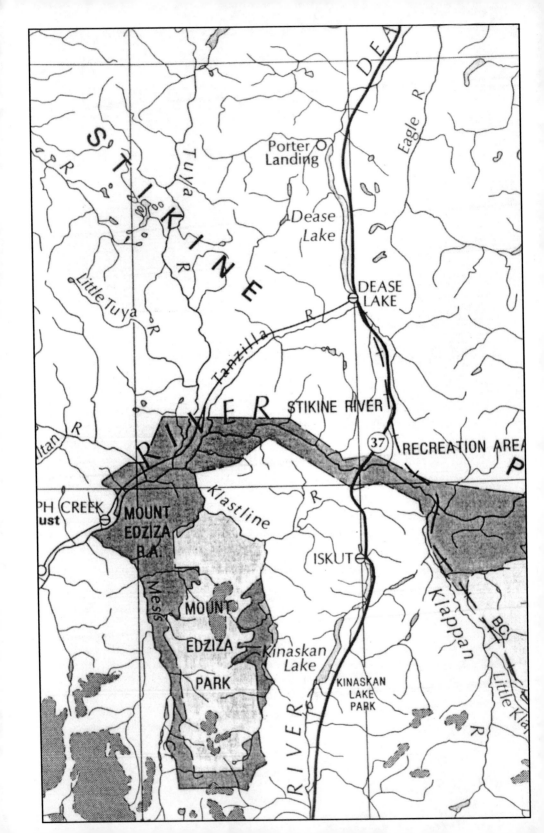

CASSIAR'S ELUSIVE GOLD

Finding gold in the wilds of Northern British Columbia was one thing. Getting the gold to the bank was quite another.

FRANCIS E. CALDWELL

Prologue

Joe Krause of Ketchikan, Alaska, had a problem. He'd been told where a fabulously rich placer gold deposit was located, but reaching the wild, remote area was beyond his capabilities.

It began after he befriended an old, crippled miner by the name of "Scotty." On his deathbed, Scotty presented Joe with a crude, aged map, showed him several nuggets and told him the story how he and his partner, Cass, had discovered a rich placer mine in the wilds of northern British Columbia a decade before the Klondike Gold Rush.

They had picked up a fortune in nuggets and dust with their fingers and a rocker before an early fall blizzard closed the passes and drove them out of the mountains. Both pack mules died. Weighted down by gold and camp equipment, they began a long trek over unknown territory to Telegraph Creek, and became hopelessly lost. Winter set in. Cass froze his feet and was unable to continue. Scotty left Cass and his share of the gold with the first people they encountered, a Tahltan Indian trapper.

Scotty managed to reach Victoria, British Columbia, the nearest hospital, paying a terrible price escaping the North, with crippling amputations of one leg, fingers and toes. In the spring he returned to Telegraph Creek hoping to find his partner, but Cass, nor his gold, were ever found. Unable to travel the rugged wilderness, Scotty kept his mine secret.

1

Now that Joe had Scotty's map, it seemed, at first, simple enough to go into the Canadian wilds, find the mine and make his fortune. But the more Joe researched the situation, the more daunting such an undertaking became.

He needed a companion he could trust, a good outfit, and enough money to finance the trip. He had none of those things. In addition, Americans could not stake mining claims in Canada, unless they had a Canadian partner with a majority share in the company. Well, he reasoned, first he'd relocate the mine, then worry about finding a Canadian partner.

The more Joe investigated, the more difficult the project became, and the more he respected Scotty and Cass for their nerve and ability to prospect in such a remote, unexplored part of British Columbia decades previously.

The area where he needed to go remained unsurveyed, a blank place on the maps, where gold nuggets nestled amongst gravel on a mountainside. It was disturbing knowledge.

Joe bided his time, hoping for a solution. Then, in the 1920s, a few small airplanes began showing up in Alaska. He decided flying into the wilderness would solve his transportation problems.

He located a plane, but before he could make his move, the airplane crashed.

◆ ◆ ◆

The possibility of discovering gold weighed heavily upon men's minds during the eighteen hundreds, especially the latter part of the century. People all over the world suffered from a series of global depressions. There were no welfare programs. If they happened to live where there was a soup kitchen, or could raise, catch or hunt something to eat, they were fortunate. Otherwise, they went hungry. It was a desperate time.

The promise of quick wealth in the western gold fields motivated tens of thousands of men, and a surprising number of women, to leave the comforts of home, loved ones and families and join various gold rushes, always west, then north, to California, Deadwood, Dakota Territory, Virginia City, Montana Territory, then north, to the Queen Charlotte Islands, the Fraser River, Cariboo, then farther north, to the wild, remote Cassiar District, where our story takes place. Gold was also discovered at Lituya Bay, Territory of Alaska, in 1880, then, later, in the Atlin District, of wild, unexplored northern British Columbia, at the same time gold was discovered in the Klondike, Yukon Territory. But I am getting ahead of my story.

Thus prospectors and miners, pushing back the frontier, became the vanguard for permanent settlements. The gold finds were seldom located in easily reached places. It took an incredibly tough breed of human to even reach most of the area, let alone dig for gold after they arrived. Some of these settlements survived. A few, like Barkerville, became modern-day tourist attractions. Most reverted back to wilderness after the gold disappeared. Today many are impossible to locate, overgrown with weeds and trees, the crude cabins rotting hulks, smashed flat by countless winter snows, the "diggings" filled in by floods or dredges that followed the early-day miner.

Political boundaries between northern British Columbia, Southeast Alaska and the Yukon were mostly unknown, and universally ignored, at the time this story begins in 1874. Even during the Klondike Gold Rush of 1897-1898, it was uncertain, for a time, whether the strike was in the newly purchased Territory of Alaska, the Yukon Territory or British Columbia. Most Americans simply assumed the Klondike was in Alaska. Frankly, few cared, except, perhaps, the Canadian government, in the form of the Royal Canadian Mounted Police and Gold Commission. Well into the late Nineteenth Century, Canadians and Americans mingled freely, working in each other's countries without restrictions or permits, ignoring physical political boundaries.

Placer gold was considered, to the uninitiated, "free" for the taking. But the experienced miners knew gold was seldom free. Any man willing to suffer the hardships of the stampede trail, if indeed a trail existed, put up the money for a grubstake, provided he arrived at the strike while good ground remained, could stake his claim and attempt to make his fortune. The physical, emotional and dollars price of reaching the gold fields was often too great, especially for people who were not accustomed to "roughing it." People who had never previously camped out a single night in the woods, unaccustomed to living with only canvas for shelter in bitter cold. People with feet too tender to walk through rough country with heavy packs strapped to their backs. For the dangers of the northern wilderness were not to be ignored. Many died of malnutrition, scurvy, disease and exposure. Thousands became discouraged, unable to withstand the hardships, and turned back short of the gold fields. A surprising number reached the gold fields only to look around in confusion at the strange scene, wondered why they'd came and departed without even trying to stake a claim.

Tent and shack cities sprang up like mushrooms on a damp, fall day. Then, when word of a new, and "possibly" better strike filtered through the wilderness grapevine, abruptly disappeared as swiftly as snow in July.

No serious prospector could afford to miss "rushing," or "stampeding," to new locations. Until the new ground was tested, there was always the possibility that it might turn out to be the richest find ever. To have known about the find, and missed it, would have been despairing, to say the least, especially for the professional miner. Captain William Moore had been so devastated when he missed the California gold strikes, he vowed he'd never miss another, and for half a century didn't.

Basically three types of people followed the gold: The experienced miners, men that had prospected and mined in Australia, South Africa, California and other western states and provinces. They were, as one can imagine, a hardy, freedom-loving breed. Most were hard working and honest, observed the Miners Code and Creed, and respected impromptu Miner's Courts, frequently the only justice and law, until official law reached the far-flung mining camps.

The second types were the "boomers," the shoe and bank clerks, the farmers, the adventure-struck and the down-and-out who had nothing to lose, except their grubstakes, and, of course, their lives!

The third type were not miners, or even "boomers'" but professional camp followers, the prostitutes, gamblers, con men, saloon keepers, storekeepers, river boat men and those wanting to be at the location of the action. In many instances they were the ones who struck it rich, coming out with more gold than those who dug it.

The scene of this gold strike was the Province of British Columbia, formed in 1858, a great producer of metals. Gold was first discovered in 1852 at Englefield Harbor, on the wild west coast of Moresby Island in the Queen Charlotte Group. Eight years later gold was found on bars along the Fraser River and Forts Hope and Yale were built to protect miners and merchants from the Indians. By 1860 miners had advanced up the Fraser as far as practical to travel with steam-powered river boats of the time. Some had managed to reach the upper river over trails clinging to the cliffs along terrible canyons. Eventually the impossible Fraser River Canyon was bypassed by the Harrison-Lillooet Trail and the rush into the interior was on.

Cariboo Lake and Horsefly Rivers became known to miners throughout the world. But two men, Keithley and Weaver, with two companions, weren't satisfied with Cariboo Lake. They found gold on a stream flowing into Cariboo Lake, and a camp, as well as the stream, were named Keithley. True prospectors, Keithley and Weaver didn't stop long but continued over the divide into an untouched valley and stumbled upon gravel running $75 to $100 a pan! This creek was named Antler Creek.

With each new strike richer than the previous, intense excitement occurred. The richest of all was found in 1862 by Billy Barker and John Cameron. Barkerville, now a famous ghost town, was unbelievably rich. The gold was deep, 50-60 feet, and at 52 feet Barker found gravel producing $1000 per square foot! When word of Barkerville reached the world an unimaginable mad stampede resulted. Our two prospectors, Scotty and Cass, were there in the thick of the Cariboo gold strikes. Exactly where we don't know.

The Cariboo District produced an enormous amount of gold, estimated at $2.5 million in 1861. Few believed that official figure. Many miners were so afraid of being robbed they never declared their finds, preferring to hide it away under stumps in fruit jars instead of trusting it to transport over the dangerous trails to a bank on the Lower Mainland. Many believe $5 million would be more accurate, an enormous amount of money then.

Like all gold placer fields, it didn't take long for the big companies to move in with their heavy equipment, the signal for prospectors to move on. Many moved to the little-known Stikine River, then into the vast, remote Stikine Plateau of Northern British Columbia, to become known as the Cassiar District. This is a huge, wilderness area that lies south of the Alaska Highway and was recently bisected by Cassiar Highway 37, completed in 1972. West of the Plateau lays an area of still unexplored glaciers amidst the high, snow-covered Coast Mountains.

Because of its remoteness, and difficult access, the Stikine Plateau and Atlin Lake areas remained one of the last places in Northern British Columbia to become explored and accurately mapped. Not until the recent use of aerial photography for mapping did anyone know what much of this remote wilderness contained. Even then, unraveling its labyrinth of rivers, creeks and watershed was a daunting task. It's important to provide some historical background and inform the reader of the difficulties of traveling through this region during the late 1800s. We have the advantage of seeing this region through the eyes of Captain Moore, and Scotty and Cass, as they struggled overland from Telegraph Creek to Dease Lake, over the same trail Captain William Moore and his three sons had traveled in 1873 to reach and stake claims on Thibert and Dease Creeks.

Before the Alaska Highway was completed, in November 1942, transportation into northern British Columbia was limited almost exclusively to either river travel (over the ice with sleds during winter and with boats during summer) or horse and mule pack trains. During summer the country was a sea of bogs and swamps that would swallow a packhorse. During the winter travel was easier with swamps, lakes and rivers frozen, but killing cold was a problem for anyone on the move. Only two rivers, the Fraser and Columbia, penetrated into north central British Columbia, and the currents and canyons of both prevented uninterrupted transport.

Consequently, any river that penetrated through the rugged Coast Range and reached the interior, farther up the coast than the Fraser, were especially valuable as a means of access to this mostly unknown territory. Included are the Skeena, Stikine, Taku and Alsek. All presented tremendous problems for any river traveler. None were easy to ascend.

Most of these wild rivers terminated in the maze of channels of either the rugged Alexander's Archipelago of Southeast Alaska or the deep fiords of northern British Columbia.

Native people, both coastal and interior tribes, having lived there for centuries, were the first to know and use the rivers as highways into the interior. During the brief summer, if the current wasn't too strong, they sailed, paddled or poled their dugout canoes upstream. They also traveled over river ice with snowshoes and pack or sled dogs during the winter.

One peculiar, and confusing geographic aspect of the Stikine Plateau is because it sits astride the Arctic Divide, and sends its waters into four major watersheds, the Yukon and Mackenzie Rivers to the north, the Peace, which eventually empties into Hudson's Bay, and the Stikine and Taku Rivers, that empty some 200 kilometers apart, into the Pacific Ocean. The network of smaller tributaries of these major rivers that head on the Plateau, especially in the section north of the Stikine River, flow in every which direction, encircling it like an octopus's tentacles.

Some waters flow into the Jennings and Teslin rivers, both emptying into Teslin Lake, which drains into the Yukon River and

Bering Sea. Others flow into the Little Rancheria, Cottonwood Creek, the Laird and thus the Mackenzie and the Arctic Ocean. The Nahlin and the Inklin empty into the Taku and the Pacific Ocean at Taku Inlet near Juneau, Alaska. Others flow into the Tuya and mighty Stikine River, a watershed encompassing 20,000 square miles, which also empties into the Pacific at Wrangell, Alaska.

Imagine an old, Sitka spruce tree, notorious for having shallow roots, with large and small roots spreading out in all directions. Turn that tree upside down, and you have a description of the many waterways draining the Stikine Plateau .

That's the description of the northern part of the Stikine Plateau, now called the Tanzilla, Taku and Kawdy Plateaus, lying north of the Stikine River. To the South, more watersheds, frustrated because the Coast Range blocks access to the sea, form a spider work of drainages, the Iskut, Klappan, Mess Creek and other rivers. Much of this country is still largely unexplored, except by air, and a considerable portion is locked in perpetual snow and glacier ice.

It's a miracle that men unraveled as much of this amazing wilderness and its major rivers as they did, prior to the use of aircraft. The Natives knew much of the country through trapping expeditions. Although certain places were too inaccessible, or they had no reason to go there. Indian trappers certainly penetrated part of the Plateau during the winter with either pack or dog sleds. It's interesting to conclude, that without the First Nation people's knowledge, passed on to white men, exploration of much of the American West and Canadian North would have been set back half a century. An example is the assistance provided to Lewis and Clark by several Native tribes.

Imagine following the headwaters of a newly-discovered river found in the Interior, as Alexander Mackenzie and his party had in 1793, when he came upon the headwaters of the Fraser River, which he mistakenly though was the Columbia River. When it became impassable he struck out overland and 13 days later reached the coast near Bella Coola where he wrote upon a large rock the famous message, "Alexander Mackenzie, from Canada, by land, the twenty-second of July, one thousand seven hundred and ninety-three." Almost all river exploration was carried out from their mouths inland.

To add to other daily obstacles in early-day north country travel, besides the lack of maps, were mosquitos, black flies, impassable canyons, bogs and swamps, running out of supplies and the danger of either losing one's supplies, having them stolen or being attack by black or grizzly bears. Grizzlies, especially those living along the Stikine River, were especially unpredictable. The very first grizzly this writer saw was from the safety of a tree stand while hunting moose along the Iskut River. It appeared as big as a horse! Last, but by no means least, was the possibility of being attack by Indians, and we have several accounts of that happening. The whites were usually better armed, so the conflicts didn't amount to much. Early during the Fraser River gold rush there were many battles between whites and Indians, and the Indians sometimes used rattlesnake poison on their arrow heads.

Tahltan, Inland Tlingit and Cascas people inhabited the Stikine Plateau, but settled mostly along major rivers, where they had trapped and hunted for centuries. The Natives believed that certain localities were inhabited by bad spirits, the *Kucda quani*, the Land Otter People. The Great Spirit did not want people to go there, perhaps relatives or friends had ventured into those areas and never returned. It is a land where people could wander aimlessly, especially if lost, until they died. Our miners, Scotty and Cass, were to discover why the Natives avoided part of the region.

Two major westward-flowing rivers, that concern us in this story, breach the rugged Coast Range and unfurl their tributaries onto the Stikine Plateau; the Taku, just south of Juneau, and the Stikine at Wrangell, about 100 miles to the south. Other watersheds flow east, or north, away from the Pacific. Both the Taku and Stikine river systems share a curious trait; they enter the mountains in an easterly direction, then veer unexplainably to the south, causing original explorers no end of difficulty.

THE TAKU RIVER:

Vessels belonging to the Russian-American Company arrived at the mouth of the Taku River in the 1700s looking for furs. Powerful Taku chiefs jealously controlled all trade with the interior tribes. Not until after seeing Russian trade goods, beads, iron, cooking pots and calico, and probably arms and ammunition, did they decide trade with white men would provide them with even more goods to barter with the interior people. Amazingly, the Taku chiefs allowed the Russians access into the Taku, as far as navigation was practical. The Russians built a well-constructed fort, supposedly in 1841 at "Tako" at the forks of the Taku and Inklin Rivers. This building, containing a cannon, survived into modern times but the cannon has been stolen. Some of the Natives of this region, including Taku Chief Aannyatlahaash, spoke limited Russian.

Russian miners may have followed Indian trails inland from "Tako" Fort to the vicinity of Atlin Lake half a century before known white prospectors. Evidence (a rotten cabin, 30-year-old musket, a skeleton and 30kg of gold dust) were discovered by miners on "Musket," now Boulder Creek, in 1898. Although 80 miles in length, Atlin Lake was not placed on the maps until after George M. Dawson's exploration of the area in 1878. He heard from the Tlingit that a large lake existed in the area, but did not find it, although he did establish the fact that it drained into the Yukon River, a good example of the improbabilities of wilderness exploration.

It was the Taku River that attracted the first attention of whites attempting to penetrate the interior. In 1866-67 Michael Byrne, employed by the Western Union Overland Telegraph Company, whose goal was to lay wire from America to Europe, traveled through the region. There is some speculation about exactly where and how much he traveled, because his reports, by some estimates, omit vital details. Construction was started in 1865, reached the confluence of the Kispiox and Skeena Rivers, then ended after the Trans-Atlantic cable was laid.

After Taku Natives carrying placer gold nuggets arrived at New Archangle (Sitka) the nearest trading post at the time, in 1866 and 1867, they were followed home by prospectors.

The Taku-Juneau area is well mineralized. Several productive and famous mines, the Alaska Juneau and Treadwell, the latter supposedly the richest lode mine ever found in Alaska, were eventually located along either side of Gastineau Channel, and Tulsequah was located up the Taku River.

Lieutenant Schwatka, exploring the Taku area in 1892, reported there were three Native trails from the head of navigation, 50 miles upriver, leading into the interior. One trail led to Atlin Lake, one led, roundabout, to Teslin Lake and the third went up the Inklin River to the Sheslay River, then up Kakuchuya Creek and Hackett River to Connect Lake, over a divide to the Little Tahltan River and southeast down that to Tahltan Village at the confluence of the Tahltan and Stikine Rivers, 10 miles above Telegraph Creek. This is roughly 210 kilometers, or 130 miles. Some of those names did not exist during the 1800s, but can be found on modern Northwestern British Columbia map 1BL.

Native trails left something to be desired, and many were little more than game trails, although they built some remarkable bridges, as will be mentioned later. Without saws and iron axes to cut out fallen timber, they had to go around windfalls. To blaze the trail Native travelers used some ingenious methods, including simply breaking off limbs, tied limbs in knots, building rock cairns or other simple methods. Some trails were fit only for summer, while others depended upon frozen lakes and streams and were only suitable during the winter.

There was commerce between the interior and coastal tribes, mostly furs, copper, gold, porcupine quills, and dried berries from the interior, fish oil, salmon from the coast for centuries. Later, after Europeans arrived in southeast Alaska in the late 1700s. Captain George Vancouver reported no less than 20 vessels, hailing from several countries, were engaged in the Northwest fur trade during his visit in 1792. The Russian-American Company arrived

Tahltan Village, confluence of Tahltan and Stikine rivers.

in Southeast Alaska in 1799. Trade goods obtained from Russians and other nations began to show up throughout southeastern Alaska and northern British Columbia in possession of Natives.

CHINESE INFLUENCE: Evidence exists that the Chinese made landfall in Southeast Alaska before the time of Christ. Were they sailors blown into the Pacific by a typhoon, then making landfall in Alaska? Taku, not a native Tlingit word, appears at a place on the Gulf of Chihli, just below Tientsis, not far from Beijing on the Chinese mainland and again in the Gambier Islands of the South Pacific.

Could Chinese have penetrated into the Cassiar? Perhaps a better question is, why would they have chosen such an inhospitable, inaccessible wilderness?

According to an article in **The Victoria Daily Colonist**, (1883) miners, while excavating gravel in the Cassiar, discovered Chinese coins buried several feet deep. There were no surface indications that the ground had previously been disturbed. The coins were brought to Victoria and shown to Chinese experts, who claimed they bore a date 1,200 years before Christ!

It's also been reported that Natives of this area, especially the Casca, who's homeland was north and east of that of the Tahltans, resembled the Mongolian race more so than other tribes living in Southeast Alaska and northern British Columbia.

Whatever their origins, the Tahltan, and the Inland Tlingit who claimed most of the Stikine River drainage from the Iskut to its headwaters and as far south as the headwaters of the Nass River, were known for their extraordinary size and prodigious strength. Both belong to the D'en'e branch of the Athabascan family division known as the Nahani.

THE STIKINE RIVER: This 400-mile-long river drains 20,000-square-miles and is actually two rivers, the Upper and Lower. Several major tributaries, including the Tuya and Iskut, swell the lower river until at its mouth it spreads out into shallow channels with dangerous, shallow sand bars many miles wide.

Some 200 miles from its mouth lies the 60-mile-long, 1,000-foot-deep Grand Canyon, a gorge so inaccessible it has not been explored, except by air. The gradient is so swift (40 feet per mile average) that Pacific salmon cannot ascend. This, and the impass-able canyon on the Iskut, are two northern river rapids no white-water kayaker has, to this writer's knowledge, yet dared descend.

Another peculiar aspect of the Stikine, already mentioned, is its abrupt change in direction. From its mouth to the beginning of the Grand Canyon the river trends north and east, then mysteriously circles around, like a dog grabbing for its tail, continues east, then, to further confuse the geographer, hooks abruptly south, heading near Tuaton Lake, on the Spatsizi Plateau. Tuaton Lake is only about 25 airline miles from the headwaters of the Nass River. The latter flows into Portland Canal near Prince Rupert. The Stikine's major tributary, the rip roaring but usually clear Iskut, bisects the huge curve of the Stikine, like an drawn arrow on a bow. Its head-waters are only a few miles from the Stikine in the vicinity of the south end of the Grand Canyon.

Exactly how surveyors and explorers ever sorted through most of this jigsaw puzzle of rivers, before aerial mapping, is an amazing story in itself. They did a remarkable job.

For its first 145 miles, to Glenora, the Stikine was claimed by both the fierce coastal Tlingit of Wrangell and the Tahltan, in a curious treaty described by George Emmonds that allowed the Tlingit access to the river during the summer, and the Tahltan during the winter. The Tahltan frequently trapped the Iskut, coming down the river on the ice. The reason for such an agreement was thought to be because coastal Tlingit traveled by canoe, while the Tahltan were not boatmen and traveled with dogs and backpacks.

River boat traffic on the Stikine has a rich history that lasted over a century, limited, of course, to the ice-free summer. The first paddle wheel steamer to ascend the Stikine and actually reach Telegraph Creek was Captain William Moore's beloved *Gertrude*, specially shallow-built, 120 feet in length, and with 10 watertight compartments in case she was holed by submerged logs on the treacherous Stikine. River boats were sometimes forced to winch through through Little Canyon, so narrow captains blew their steam whistle before entering, fearful of meeting another vessel. And other vessels there soon were, as we shall mention later.

In 1898, during the Klondike Gold Rush, the Stikine was chosen as a route to the Yukon instead of Chilkoot Pass at the head of Lynn Canal. Consequently, much has been published about the difficulties of ascending the Stikine, and then reaching Yukon headwaters over some of the worst trails in the north.

Englishman Guy Lawrence, aged 17, came to Canada with his father in 1898, 13 years after our story begins, intending on using this route to Dawson. Like many other stampeders, they were victims of inaccurate information, rampant during the Klondike Gold Rush. They'd been told before leaving England that a wagon road was nearly complete between Telegraph Creek and Teslin Lake. Their experiences, described in 40 YEARS ON THE YUKON TELEGRAPH, are a wealth of information about the area this story deals with.

Chief Shakes canoe along the Stikine River. Chief Shakes was the Tlingit chief from Wrangell.

I repeat some of Lawrence's experiences on the Atlin Trail and Telegraph Trail, and later in the story, those of Captain William Moore and his sons, who backpacked from Telegraph Creek to Dease Lake over what would later become the Moore trail, during the start of the Cassiar Gold Rush. Both are vivid examples of the difficulties experienced while traveling during the late 1800s in northern British Columbia. Lawrence recorded many disasters where men lost limbs to the cold, froze to death on the trail, starved or died of scurvy, through carelessness, inexperience and disregard for the weather.

The Lawrences reached Wrangell during the early spring, while the Stikine was still encased in ice down to its mouth. Wrangell was a rip-roaring boom town, with hundreds of tents, a few dance halls, saloons and a handful of confidence men who had fled Skagway after Soapy Smith had been shot. They hired a carpenter to build a small, flat-bottom river boat, then moved camp to Cottonwood Island, where they waited six weeks for the ice to go out. They gave up trying to row or sail up the river after only a few miles and drifted back down to Cottonwood Island, where they spent another of seven weeks attempting to catch a ride on one of many river boats passing by. One boat, the *Monte Cristo*, claimed they had no room for passengers because they were loaded with 30 tons of hard liquor destined for thirsty miners. Finally the *Skagit Chief*, piloted by Captain A.W. Gray, picked them up. The *Skagit Chief* had been built in Tacoma, Washington in 1887, and was 137.5 feet long, with a 26.3 foot beam and had operated around Puget Sound until the Klondike rush sent her north in May, 1898.

Lawrence describes the power of the Stikine, which he claims can rise 20 feet in one day. The ancient, underpowered *Skagit Chief* reached Little Canyon, but couldn't make it through because the current was too swift.

For nine agonizing days they tied up to the bank below the canyon, watching other more powerful boats whiz by. Finally, the stern wheeler *Stikine Chief* took them on board and they reached the tent city of Glenora, where 4,500 impatient stampeders milled in confusion because the government had canceled the Teslin wagon road contract. Instead, a four-foot-wide trail had been built.

Since most had relied on getting their supplies hauled to Teslin Lake by wagons, this was a bitter disappointment. Two professional pack trains operated between Glenora and Teslin Lake, but the price was 57 cent a pound. It would cost over $1000 to transport their required ton of goods, too much for most. Since no horses were available, the next best option was to backpack. If they could pack 60 pounds, that meant 33 round trips, or almost 8,000 miles of trekking for a distance of 230 miles through the wilderness.

The packers got rich. Many stampeders sold their outfits for enough to buy passage home. One man was making a fortune buying and shipping unwanted supplies back south.

The good news was a large pack train was en route from Edmonton, 1,400 miles away! The horses arrived at the end of July. One can well imagine the sorry state the animals were in after a forced, overland march that far. Most were so poor and stove up they sold for $5.

Eventually the Lawrence's bought a horse, made a cart, and proceeded to relay their equipment 36 miles to the Tahltan River,

With their belongings on a two-wheeled cart, these men are on the Teslin Lake Trail between the Stikine and Teslin Lake. c.1897

where others had already built cabins and holed up for the winter. In mid-October, with deep snow and severe cold, they also built a cabin and spent the winter. The horse became dog food.

At Tahltan, they learned of a gold strike at Atlin, 230 miles away, over the nearly impossible Atlin Trail, not recommended by anyone who had been over it. There was another way to reach Atlin, via the Teslin trail. Since Atlin was 800 miles closer than the Klondike, they changed plans and headed for Teslin Lake in mid- February, one year after sailing from England, towing sleds loaded with their remaining supplies. The pass between Tahltan and Teslin was 4,400 feet in elevation. Perhaps 4,400 feet elevation doesn't sound very intimidating to most readers unfamiliar with the sub-arctic. In the Interior, at Latitude 58 Degrees North, temperatures frequently dropped to 40 or 50 degrees below zero.

One evening, at Long Lake, they came upon what appeared to be an abandoned log hut. No tracks in the snow were visible and no smoke came from the stovepipe. Anticipating spending a comfortable, warm night for a change, they pushed inside. Two bunks, one above the other, lined the back wall. Each bunk contained a body, frozen stiff in their blankets, dead from scurvy. The Lawrences spent the night in their tent! Although the tent caught fire around the stove pipe, even during the blaze a thermometer inside registered 44 degrees below zero, according to Mr. Lawrence!

At Teslin Lake, a large barge was being build to head for Dawson after the ice went out. But the Lawrence's were not headed for Dawson. A formidable trip to Atlin still lay ahead. After towing sleds 30 miles down Teslin Lake, the trail turned west along a chain of small frozen lakes for 100 miles until they reached the south end of Atlin Lake, the largest in British Columbia. Then they walked the ice 26 miles to Atlin.

Guy Lawrence's father only stayed a short time in Atlin before returning home to England. Guy worked several years in mines around Atlin, then joined the Yukon Telegraph Line. In 1902.

By late fall, 1901, 1,900 miles of telegraph wire had been strung between Ashcroft, British Columbia and Dawson City, Yukon Territory, and the line passed near Atlin. Men were stationed at 38 stations, spaced at intervals along this remote route to maintain the wire. Some of the stations were over 100 miles from any town.

Between Telegraph Creek and Atlin Lake were three stations, Nakina, Nahlin and Sheslay. Mr. Lawrence served at both Nakina and Nahlin, an area west of the location of the Fishhook Lake Mine. While at Nahlin Station, he discovered some rich gold float that could be a clue to the source of the Fishhook Lake Mine. More about this later.

No Native trail existed from its mouth up the Stikine river to head of navigation. This is some of the toughest walking imaginable. The country is so difficult a proposed road down the Stikine, that would have provided Canada with a much needed seaport, failed to happen. This road was considered by both governments during the 1960s. Alaska, more optimistic, and flush with oil revenue, completed the short Alaska section, the Mitkoff Highway from Petersburg to the mouth of the river. The Canadian Government, perhaps wiser and definitely poorer, never started their section. It would have been a daunting and expensive project, prone to winter avalanche and summer floods. The Telegraph Road would have needed improvement also. Some of the toughest walking experienced by this writer was along the Stikine.

Atlin Lake, the Stikine River Valley and Cassiar Mining District all have their prehistoric mysteries. I've already mentioned the unexplainable, 3000-year-old Chinese coins found at Dease Lake. Another mystery is dozens of ancient rock cairns along the mountainsides upriver from the U.S./ Canada border along the Stikine. They are most abundant upriver from Scud River. The cairns are about three feet high, the same diameter. They are very old. Perhaps they were used as "markers" by Natives sometime in the distant past. But markers for what?

TRADING POSTS AND HOOCHINOO: One of the first white traders to penetrate the Stikine country was Al "Buck" Choquette who established a trading post 145 miles upriver, at Glenora, about 1870. He was also responsible for the first Stikine stampede at Buck's Bar. The history of the Stikine gold strike came about in this way.

Captain Moore had been bouncing back and forth up and down the coast on every navigable river between the Fraser and Stikine Rivers since the 1860s, depending upon where the current action was. He had also looked over the Taku River, and decided it was useless, with no harbor at its mouth, and dangerous, infamous "Taku winds" frequently blowing out of the interior with tremendous force.

In 1861 word filtered down the coast that Alexander "Buck" Choquette had found gold on a bar far up the Stikine River in Southeast Alaska. Not one to miss out on a new discovery, in the late spring of 1862 Moore had ran the *SS Flying Dutchman* a 92-foot paddle wheel steamer built in 1861 at Victoria, towing the barge *J.W. Moore*, up the Inside Passage to Fort Wrangell. Alaska was still owned by Russia, but of course Captain Moore never bothered asking permission to enter Alaska. Not one navigational aid was in place between the Fraser River and Wrangell, a perilous voyage of about 600 miles. On board were 125 eager prospectors, plus cargo. A Tlingit river pilot was taken on board at Fort Wrangell. This is believed to have been the first river boat on the Stikine River.

On this trip up the river, the Tlingit accosted Captain Moore and told him he could not run his fireboats up their river any longer because they would frighten away the fish and game. Moore negotiated a settlement, $200 worth of Hudson Bay blankets, and peace was restored. Buck's Bar, and three other nearby bars, were tough to work during the melt-off, or high water, and quickly fizzled out. At best they produced only $3 to $10 per man per day.

While miners didn't get rich that season, Captain Moore made $20,000 with his boat. Other big happenings were brewing on the Stikine that would provide lots of business for river boats. The Overland Telegraph Expedition intended to lay wire connecting North America and Europe. The line would pass through British Columbia and Alaska, then cross Bering Straits and through Russia to Europe. An ambitious project indeed. Naturally, such a project required a massive amount of equipment and manpower. The entire route was almost totally unknown wilderness. A large river boat, the *Mumford*, built at Victoria for the company was loaded with freight and ascended the Stikine as far as possible, where the wire was to cross the river, a location to become known as Telegraph Creek. Before the project got started the Trans-Atlantic cable was laid and the entire scheme was abandoned. Hundreds of tons of wire and freight were hauled back south.

Both Glenora and Telegraph Creek became strategic locations. Glenora as the start of the infamous Teslin Trail. Telegraph Creek as head of navigation for steamboats and start of the Moore Trail to Dease Lake Landing. Hudson's Bay Company had a small post at Glenora as early as 1874, but the post was abandoned because of a lack of business in 1876. During the boom years of 1898 it was reestablished, but by 1902 was abandoned again in favor of Telegraph Creek. The Hudson's Bay Company trading post operated by Choquette flourished. He became fluent in the native language, and later built a second store, the Hudson's Bay Company's Post, at the U.S./Canadian Boundary.

Hudson's Bay Company policy was to refuse selling alcohol to the natives. Choquette, and probably others, ignored orders. Examination of shipments of freight to the north during this period would undoubtedly have indicated a larger than appropriate amount of molasses, potatoes, brown sugar and yeast, essential ingredients in making "hootch". Trafficking in whiskey with the natives was a serious offence in Canada. Choquette was hauled into court for his crime.

The Natives quickly became proficient at making their own "hootchnioo" and went into the liquor business big time, selling to both races.

Another Canadian, independent trader John Calbreath, established a trading post at Teslin Lake in 1886, then later at Telegraph Creek. He advertised in the Times Colonist that he could place goods at his Teslin Lake post at a cost of $250 per ton, by shipping up the Stikine and overland with horses on the Teslin Trail.

Navigable rivers and established trails eventually became known to the whites, but many surrounding rugged, snowy mountains, plateaus and wild nameless rivers remained *terra incognito* at the time our two brave, hearty, foot-loose miners arrived in 1874.

At the time our story begins, the Territory of Alaska had been in possession of the United States only seven years. The white population of the Territory was estimated to number only 2,000.

Basically, this is a true story. I knew two of the main characters very well. One was my neighbor, the other my boss for several years. I've stuck to as many facts as possible, fictionalized and seasoned the tale with dialogue to make it more readable and understandable. Naturally, this writer cannot know what men said to each other a century ago. Research was gleaned from trips to northern British Columbia, the Yukon and various documents and publications (see Bibliography)

You may call it historical fiction, or "fraction." Whatever you label it, this tale deserves telling. It's a story about human endurance, exploration and the passion some men had for finding riches in the Northern Gold Fields.

Chapter One

✦

The Wild Cassiar Country

The characters in this story, Scotty and Cass, discoverers of the Fishhook Lake Mine, were seasoned, experienced placer miners. They had cut their teeth on the Fraser River gold strikes, then moved to the Big Bend of the Columbia River, survived the great Canadian smallpox epidemic of 1862, then made a small fortune in the Cariboo District at Barkerville by 1866. It was here in this rip roaring boom town they met Captain William Moore, who was living in a house nearby with his family during the winter. Moore was already a legendary pioneer river boat captain and ship owner who they would come to know well during the next few years.

With no new strikes in the wind, they had, on a whim, "rushed", with a lot of other Canadians and Americans, to South Africa upon news of a fabulous strike in the Rand. They didn't go broke in Africa, as many did. They spent several years exploring and mining in the Transvaal with disappointing results. Discouraged and homesick, they embarked on a ship for the British Isles, then another for New York and headed home for British Columbia.

When they left British Columbia, Victoria had been only a tiny village surrounding the eastern half of the Inner Harbor. Cows, pigs and goats vied with pedestrians and horses for right of way in the narrow streets. To their amazement, the town had been transformed into a booming city, with shipyards, breweries and outfitting stores galore.

Their money running low, they were looking for new diggings.

I cannot tell you much about either miner. Both were in their late twenties or early thirties and single. Scotty was described as a short, powerful, sandy-haired man, a transplanted Scotsman, with a sense of humor. Of his partner, Cass, we know even less, except he was a big, rugged, fun-loving character, never one to pass up a fight. Like many early-day miners, he was Irish. Both men's philosophy fit the classic description of the genuine, old-time prospector:

> "There's gold, and it's haunting and haunting;
>   It's luring me on as of old;
> Yet it isn't the gold that I'm wanting
>   So much as just finding the gold.
> It's a great, big, broad land 'way up yonder,
>   It's the forests where silence has lease;
> It's the beauty that fills me with wonder,
>   It' the stillness that fills me with peace.

(ROBERT SERVICE *"THE SPELL OF THE YUKON."*)

Hardship, isolation, danger and hard work had bonded Scotty and Cass until they were compatible partners, willing to give their lives for one another. On the Stikine Plateau, that loyalty was to be tested to the utmost.

Victoria, British Columbia, in the spring of 1874, was the most important shipping port on the Northwest Coast. Scotty and his partner, Cass, before arriving in Victoria, while riding the newly constructed Union Pacific Railroad, began hearing rumors about a new gold strike at home in British Columbia.

While they had been in Africa, in 1872, men by the names of Thibert and McCullough, and the well-known Captain William Moore and his sons, had made a gold strike of great importance in the Cassiar District of Northern B.C.

"Wouldn't you know," said Scotty to his partner, Cass, "While we were off to the ends of the earth looking for gold, someone found more of it right here under our noses in Canada!"

Cass countered with, "Had we not gone to Africa we would never have known Francine and Ursula."

A sigh. "You're right. They are unforgettable. But, until we get to the Cassiar and find out how rich our friends have became during our absence, I think we should reserve judgement regarding how much the company of those beautiful ladies was actually worth!"

Needing to recuperate their losses as quickly as possible, they quickly outfitted with a year's supply of food and tools and booked passage to Fort Wrangell, territory of Alaska, on the *SS California*. They found themselves in good company. On board were many miners they'd known in the Cariboo, including old friend Captain William Moore and his sons Henry, Johnnie and Billy.

"Where the hell have you two been?" Captain Moore demanded.

"Vacationing, in South Africa," Scotty admitted sheepishly.

Moore, a big, bluff German, scoffed. "Well, you missed a good one. Me and my boys staked claims that are worth a fortune."

"Congratulations. It's about time you struck it rich," Cass said.

"Since I've seen you two, there was another strike way to hell and gone up country. Michael Byrnes and his partner Vital La Force discovered gold on the Omineca River. And that, my friends, is why I have a permanent bow in my back.

"We built a couple of barges at Quesnel, then me and the boys dragged them up half a dozen rivers and through several lakes 260 miles to Takla Landing on Takla Lake, to supply the Omineca camps. Then, in '71 we built the *Minnie*, a centerboard schooner, loaded her with freight, 30 men and 25 mules, and took her as far up the Skeena as we could get, left her with an Indian chief, then built a pack trail 60 miles to Takla Lake. Why is it gold is always found in the farthest, God-forsaken places in the wilderness?"

"It's because idiots like you and us go off to those places looking, didn't you know? My, you've been busy. Where's the *Minnie* now?"

"On the beach in Fort Wrangell. You want a ride? And a job? I've a contract to build a trail from Telegraph Creek to Dease Lake. There's an army of men and a mountain of freight going to Dease Lake, and I plan on building a trail and packing for my share of the gold."

"How far's that?"

"Seventy miles. Tough miles too. It took my boys and me 62 days to get from Fort Wrangell to Dease Lake. We got the *Minnie* as far as the Hudsons Bay Post, then took our little barge up by hand to Telegraph Creek. From there we backpacked several ton of supplies to Dease Lake, just me and the boys and a couple of Indian packers. That was tough. There was six to eight feet of snow along the banks of the Stikine through the Coast Range, even in late April."

Quite a crowd had gathered, as they always did when Captain Moore decided to tell of his adventures, which wasn't often. He never lost his German accent, and his friends called him the Flying Dutchman, which pleased him a lot, so much he named his 92-foot paddler wheel steamer, built in 1860 the *Flying Dutchman*. He'd lost the vessel in bankrupsy in 1863.

"The question is, is there any good ground left?" Cass asked.

Captain Moore thought for a moment. "When we pulled out last September, there was. What's happened since, I'm not sure. Men were pouring into the country. We'd washed out about $5000, but, you know, it takes a while to open up a claim." Captain Moore looked at the crowd, excused himself and slipped away, muttering they'd have plenty of time to talk later.

Rumors circulated around the ship that, according to the Victoria papers, they were too late, the good ground in the Cassiar had all been staked. But they remained optimistic. "What do newspapermen know about gold mining?" they consoled themselves.

The voyage north was uneventful. Captain Moore spent most of his time in the pilothouse of the steamer visiting with the officers, or in his stateroom, but when he mingled with the passengers, and at mess, and when he felt like talking, he was always surrounded by a crowd who hung onto every word.

Giants walked the earth in those days. Captain William Moore was one. A German by birth, Moore had gone to sea at the age of seven in the North Sea. He arrived in New Orleans about 1846, where he met his wife, Hendrika, a faithful follower for the remainder of his 50 years of wandering all over the Pacific Northwest, British Columbia and Alaska..

After sailing on the SS *Lawrence* during the Mexican War of 1848, he served on towboats on the Mississippi. With an itchy foot, the California gold strike caught his interest. With son, John, known as Johnnie or J.W., and his faithful wife in tow, he moved to San Francisco, arriving in time to see wealthy miners lavishly spending their gold, but too late to participate.

He swore he'd never be late for a gold strike again, and, with one notable exception, he wasn't.. During the next half century his itinerary reads like a geographic description of British Columbia, the Yukon and Alaska. He participated in (with steamboats, packstrings, trail building crews, his presence) or actually mined at, the Queen Charlotte Islands, Fraser River, Big Bend of the Columbia, Cariboo, Omineca, Stikine River, Cassiar, Klondike and Nome.

The biggest strike of all, the Klondike, he screwed up and ignored, although he camped overnight on the future site of Dawson City during the summer of 1896, talked to George Carmacks, and yet failed to walk a few miles and stake. More on this later.

Perhaps Captain William Moore's greatest fame came from discovering White Pass and homesteading the site of Skagway, fully a decade before the Klondike Gold Rush would bring tens of thousands of stampeders rushing pell mell through Dyea and Skagway and over White Pass, known as the "horse killer." Three thousand dead horses were scattered along the trail during the winter of 1897-98.

After missing out in California, disgruntled, Moore heard about Inca gold the Spanish had found in South America. With his family, he moved to Peru, operating a trading schooner there, where a second son, William D. was born. The second son was to follow in his father's footsteps and become one of the most famous river boat captains in British Columbia and the Yukon.

Back in California, he lived on Goat Island, now supporting the San Francisco Bay Bridge, where he and his wife raised pigs and goats. After gold was discovered on the Fraser River, Captain Moore moved to Victoria, built a cottage for his family and a 15-ton barge, the *Blue Bird*, and began hauling miners up the Fraser River. During his lifetime he would build, or own, a total of 18 vessels, including the *Western Slope*, a 156-foot-long paddle wheel steamer, used on the Fraser and Stikine Rivers. He would go bankrupt twice, but never gave up his dreams of becoming a rich steamboat man and gold miner.

Wrangell, at the time of Scotty and Cass' visit, was a raw frontier trading post and Tlingit village on Wrangell Island, four miles across from Green Point, the mouth of the Stikine River. The men pitched in and helped get the *Minnie* ready to go. Some cut firewood and others cleaned her bottom and painted.

Although conditions on the little schooner were dismal, Scotty and Cass enjoyed the trip up the Stikine River. After the Transvaal and desert of Africa, the scenery was starkly beautiful, although frightening in some ways with its wild grandeur. Glaciers spilled icebergs nearly into the river. This time they were lucky the water was low and the current manageable. They dropped off the barge at Glenora, then took the *Minnie* to Telegraph Creek and unloaded the freight. Then those who wanted horses to carry their goods returned to help the Moores with the barge load of horses.

This year, with a crew to build trail, and horses, they hoped to avoid the hard work of backpacking.

Although much of the Indian trail was suitable for horses, a lot of work still needed to be done. Moore soon put all his men, as well as all the Indians he could hire at Millers, to work. Moore intended to charge as much as the traffic would bear, even charging men with backpacks two cents a pound for walking "his" trail. The trail was rugged, little more than a game track, but miners were willing to pay a hefty fee to have their supplies loaded on horses for the grueling 70 mile trip, with many steep uphill grades.

Today, if you own a high-clearance vehicle, and the weather's okay, you can drive Telegraph Creek Road, which more or less follows the old Moore Trail. Several grades are twenty percent. Inquire at Dease Lake for weather conditions before you leave.

At Telegraph Creek Scotty and Cass met Miller, who operated a trading post there, later to be owned by pioneer outfitter John C. Calbreath.

The difficulties Moore, his three sons and six other prospectors encountered the previous season are recounted to provide the reader of an example of what men were willing to endure to reach gold. The left Fort Wrangell, towing a little barge, on April 20. When they reached Glenora there was still from four to six feet of snow on the riverbanks. They left the *Minnie* in charge of an Indian chief, and headed upriver with the barge load of freight. The deep snow caused much danger and difficulty lining the barge through Stikine Canyon. Using sails, poles, and towline, it took 12 days to reach Telegraph Creek, where Miller's Post was located.

Miller arranged for two Indians to help pack. They began relaying, carrying a load as far as they could, then walking back for another. Day after day they struggled up the trail. About 15 miles above Telegraph Creek they came to the Tahltan River. Natives had constructed a suspension bridge 75 feet long. The bridge consisted of poles, bound with withes. No nails were used. The bridge looked so insecure each time one of the men crossed he expected to crash into the icy river.

Ten miles farther they reached the Tuya River where another bridge, also built without nails, 42 feet in length, spanned a narrow place between rocky cliffs where a waterfall crashed down. No one would cross this rickety bridge, since a fall would be fatal. They spent four long, hard days building their own bridge. Twenty-eight days after leaving the boat, they reached Dease Lake, where they rested one day.

Caching their packs, they traveled light and made Millers, 70 miles, in three days! Another party had arrived, so they all headed back up the trail, relaying again. At Tuya bridge 15 Indians and their families stopped the whites, saying they could not use their trails and bridges because they would scare the game away. The whites began loading their rifles and revolvers. At this show of force, the Indians said they needed payment, so Moore gave them $20 and enough food for dinner. The Indians seemed satisfied. This second trip only took 20 days to Dease Lake. The two Indians were paid $50 for their help, and sent back with mail for Mrs. Moore.

Remember, all this work, 62 days of lining, rowing and backpacking, in rain, wind and snow, over a distance of 260 miles from Fort Wrangell, and on only the promise of finding gold!

They built a raft, then poled and rowed 24 miles to Thibert Creek. On the way they passed a promising creek, about 12 miles from Thibert Creek. The boys wanted to stop and take a pan, but Captain Moore thought they should check out Thibert Creek.

Four miles up Thibert Creek they found Henry Thibert and his partners taking out from $50 to $100 a day per man with two rockers. The new arrivals staked claims and set to work. The ground was frozen hard, and they could only make $7 average a day. Johnnie and Billie quit and returned to the creek they'd seen on the way, later known as Dease Creek. Three miles up they struck good pay and sent word to their father and brother. Soon everyone on Thibert Creek moved to Dease Creek. Moore and all three boys staked discovery claims, a total width of 600 feet for the four men. Although Henry was only 14, the miners voted that he could stake, and the decision was later upheld by the provincial government at Victoria.

Miners camp on Thibert Creek. It's obvious that placer claims, staked across the creeks in Canada, were quite small because of steep hillsides on both sides of the creek. Photo dated 1911.

All during the summer men swarmed into the new diggings. Captain Moore became desperately ill and had to quit work. Even so, when they quit and headed outside in September, they had $5000 and the four claims for their efforts. As they backpacked down the trail, Captain Moore surveyed exactly what needed to be done to turn it into a horse trail. He was determined that next season no one should have to perform the exhausting labor that they had done that year.

With horses doing part of the work, except where the trail was yet impassible, Scotty, Cass and the Moore boys finally moved their gear to Dease Lake by mid-June, and onto a barge someone had built during the winter.

Laketon was booming. The Moore boys were amazed to see dance halls and saloons springing up where last season had only been lodgepole pine and birch. Obviously a lot of work had been accomplished during the winter while they were away. Where people came from was a mystery.

Thibert Creek's rich diggings was, like countless other gold finds, discovered by accident. Henry Thibert, a Minnesota American of French descent and his Scottish partner, Angus McCullough in 1872, had been sluicing out a little gold at McCullough's Bar on the Laird River, close to where Laird Hot Springs on the Alaska highway is located today. They decided to take a break, enjoy the Indian summer weather and pole up to where Lower Post is now, then pole up the Dease River to Dease Lake to harvest some fish. Those old-timers didn't mind a lot of work, as this was quite a trip, especially against the current.

At Dease Lake an Indian told them there was a big gold strike down the Stikine at a place called Buck's Bar. Unable to resist a new strike, they left their boat at Dease Lake Landing, the west end, and snowshoed 70 miles over the Indian trail to Telegraph Creek, then on down the river to Buck's Bar. The strike was a flop and the profitable ground had already been staked. Discouraged, they, and several others, turned around and began snowshoeing over the ice back up the Stikine, intending to return to Dease Lake, catch some fish, smoke them, then float down the Dease and Laird to their diggings at McCullough's Bar.

McCullough fell through the ice on the Stikine and later died of exposure. Thibert and the others buried him as best they could and continued on. Death was a constant companion on northern trails. Where they wintered, and what they ate, is unknown, but probably at Millers trading post at the present site of Telegraph Creek.

By the time they arrived back at Dease Lake, it was spring of 1873. To their disgust, they found their boat had been stolen! Stealing a boat in the North was equal to someone stealing a horse in the early-day American West, a crime punishable by hanging. Without a boat, they had little alternative but to walk home, and, fortunately, chose the west side of the lake, prospecting, of course, as they went along. That's when they found gold on a creek later named for Thibert, and they mined there all alone during the spring of 1873, until Captain William Moore, his three sons and four other miners arrived and staked claims. A town, named Dease Town at first, then Laketon, sprang up. Exactly how word of the new strike leaked out hasn't been recorded, but some of the old-timers insisted that ravens carried news of gold discoveries with lightening speed.

At Laketon, Scotty and Cass pitched their tent behind the saloon and walked up the creek with the boys to their claims. To everyone's astonishment, claim posts were scattered along the narrow creek bottom for 21-kilometers. Men were sinking shafts and washing gold through wooden sluice boxes. The creek bed was narrow and the canyon walls steep, creating very short claims, as claims were staked across the stream, instead of lengthways to the stream as they were in Alaska.

The two miners peered into several sluice boxes. A golden tinge mixed with black, magnetic sand forming at the bottom of each riffle. The claim owners smiled and handed them a shovel, but they declined, looked despairingly at each other and continued on up the creek.

With a great deal of relief, they found the Moore's Discovery Claims intact. Billy Moore offered Scotty and Cass a "lay", a 50 foot square of gravel on their poorest-paying claim, at the rate of 50 percent, but they declined, and spent several days prospecting above without success.

All the paying ground had been staked on Dease Creek. Discouraged, they moved on to Porter's Landing, at the mouth of Thibert Creek, near the outlet of the lake. But it was the same.

Credit: B.C. Provincial Archives, #D-07666

Porter's Landing, Hudson's Bay Trading Post, outlet end of Dease Lake. c.1926

For Scotty and Cass, finding no room to stake was a tough break. But they were used to such things. One more boom camp. Centerville, at the mouth of McDame Creek, lay on down the river below Dease Lake. The Dease River, a tributary of the Laird, flows into the Mackenzie River. A black prospector, McDame, had taken $6,000 worth of gold out of McDame Creek in 30 days, setting off another rush. [In 1877 Alfred Freeman was to discover one of the largest nuggets (72 ounces, or four and a half pounds) ever located in British Columbia from this creek. Today this nugget would have a face value of about $35,000, probably more to collectors.]

After Scotty learned that 300 men were already swarming along McDame Creek they didn't even bother to look.

Scotty and Cass were not alone in their disappointment. Others that were pouring up the new Moore Trail were faced with the same situation. For some, they were not only too late, but had spent their last dime getting here and were broke. They hired out to claim owners, hoping to scrape up enough money to return home.

Rather than work for someone else, Scotty and Cass considered leaving the country, but one day they ran into Captain William Moore, who had left the trail building crew long enough to check up on his sons progress. Moore cussed them out for thinking such a thing. He insisted they should take a lay on the Moore claims, but didn't persist when they refused, knowing experienced miners preferred to work their own ground.

"Remember "Doc" Keithley and George Weaver and how they left their diggings at Cariboo Lake in '60, went over the hump and struck it rich on Antler Creek?"

"Of course we remember. We were there. A little late, but we did all right. What do you think we are? Senile?"

"Well, that's what you should do, go over that mountain there to the west. One of the Tahltans working on my trail crew told me when his grandfather was young, he used to bring back nuggets as big as peanuts from somewhere up there." Moore waved his hand towards the Cassiar Mountains. "As long as you're already outfitted for the summer, strike out north into unknown country."

"We've had enough backpacking already."

"Hell. I'll sell you two mules, if that's what's stopping you. I just bought a dozen from a man who was so broke when he reached Glenora he didn't have enough money to pay the toll on my trail."

It was a well-known fact that Captain Moore would take a miner's last dollar without any compassion, and for that he was disliked by many. It was also a rumor that Tahltan and Casca Indians frequently showed up at local trading posts with gold, and they knew nothing about mining.

Scotty and Cass mulled this over. Moore's instincts for gold were legendary, so they weighed the plan carefully, then decided, although such a venture was a long shot, it would be better than mucking gravel on Captain Moore's or some other man's claims, with little chance of making more than enough to pay their way out of the country before freeze up.

The two mules that Moore selected for them were of dubious age and notorious dispositions, according to some of Moore's crew who had struggled to get them up to Dease Lake. Before the summer ended they decided Moore should have paid them for taking the cantankerous animals off his hands!

They got their mules and outfit onto the barge and took them to Thibert Creek, where they'd been told a hunter's trail went up the gulch for several miles. Upon discovering Scotty and Cass intended to prospect new country, several stampeders requested to go along, but Scotty declined because the men were inexperienced and without a grubstake.

There were no maps of the country where they were headed, but they were accustomed to that, and woods-wise enough to navigate across country using Scotty mining compass. Scotty immediately started a crude map in his notebook.

Following the trail, they climbed clear of the cursed down timber and brush. The trail ended at a big, level meadow, with evidence that hunters had recently camped. To the south was what is now the French Range, and Mount Rath, elevation 6,234 feet. The country was just emerging from winter snow. Beautiful alpine grasslands and meadows were carpeted with purple lupine, Indian paintbrush, wild rose and horse parsnips. Small stands of stunted birch and aspen provided wood. Hoards of horse flies, mosquitos and black sox almost drove them and the mules mad. They headed north into a river valley, that they thought might be the Tuya, then decided it wasn't because it was so small. They panned each creek and were pleased that everywhere they went they could find five or ten cent pans, but never more than that. Enjoying the beautiful country, they kept wandering. Elevations in this area average about 4,000 feet, with Mount Josephine, near Tuya Lake, 6,000 feet, and Ash Mountain, near High Tuya Lake, the headwaters of the Tuya, reaching 6,971 feet. But for one reason or another they missed seeing both those lakes.

Panning each stream, following the path of least resistance for the sake of their mules, they made a leisurely trip of it. The mules saw to that. When the animals became tired they refused to continue. Curse words, clubs, whips and coaxing were useless. The mules simply balked or laid down until they felt like continuing.

Heading north over a gradual plateau, where streams were dotted with beaver dams, they couldn't have known they were entering one of North America's "mother of waters" areas, astride the Arctic Divide. From here water drains into the Teslin and Jennings Rivers, then into the Yukon, while other water drains into the Little Rancheria and Dease, and flows into the Laird, then the Mackenzie River and Arctic Ocean. Others drain into the Tuya, which empties into the Stikine River, then terminates at Wrangell. Yet other tributaries drain into the Nahlin and Inklin Rivers, which empty into the Taku River and Pacific Ocean near present-day Juneau. Totally unaware they were entering into a geographic maze, they trekked cheerfully on, confident their compass would get them back. Perhaps this confusion of waters is why the Tahltans and Inland Tlingits, who didn't own a compass, were leery of parts of the huge Plateau. They didn't see any sign that man had ever been in the area.

Scotty kept track of their wanderings so they could find their way out. It was a peculiar country, with many flat-topped buttes and curiously-shaped mountains. Some consisted mostly of shale talus, while others displayed several types of bedrock. The mountains were sprinkled throughout a large, nearly level plateau. Only by noticing the direction of the water flow in the streams did they realize they were changing watersheds, but they would have been surprised had they known the destinations of some of this water included Hudson Bay!

One sparkling clear day they let the mules rest and climbed a high mountain. Far to the west lay a massive mountain range, covered with snow and glaciers, which they assumed was the Coast Range they'd passed through on the way upriver. A herd of wild sheep watched warily from shady beds on a talus slide. Stone, a darker cousin of the Dall, and Fannin sheep were plentiful and tame. They knew them only as wild sheep. Cass shot one whenever they needed meat. The flesh was excellent.

They forded streams, running high with snow melt, some carrying glacial silt. Scotty drew the rivers and streams on his map, naming them for reference. Several were so deep and swift they had much trouble finding a place to ford.

They found no sign of anyone having been there. They wandered aimlessly, stopping to work a place if they struck colors. And colors they found, almost everywhere they dipped a pan, but it wasn't enough, so they kept moving , looking for better pay.

They roved in a great semicircle to the north and northwest, following the path of least resistance.

One day, still circling towards the northwest, they crossed another pass, far above timberline, and still deep with snow on the north slope. They named it "Caribou Pass" because a herd of those animals were feeding nearby.[1] The curious caribou, never having seen humans before, followed behind the mules and men at a distance of 70 yards. Cass shot a yearling and dressed it out. He cut off the choice meat and loaded it onto the mules.

They descended talus slides so steep the mules were forced to sit on their rumps and skid. Ahead lay a large valley containing several sparkling lakes. One of those lakes would be their night's camp, so they started down.

Cass was scouting ahead for the best route for the mules. Along the northern flanks of a steep, rocky mountain ridge he jumped a flock ptarmigan. With his muzzle-loading shotgun, he bagged several for dinner.

By the time Scotty and the mules caught up with him, he was down on his knees dressing the birds in a broad wash that curiously paralleled, instead of bisected, the mountainside, as most ravines, or washes do. Scotty watched idly while Cass cleaned the birds. Half a mile below, at the base of the mountain, he noticed

---

[1] *The Osborne caribou inhabit this region. The bulls can weigh about 700 pounds, compared with about 600 pounds for mountain caribou.*

a fishhook-shaped lake, and decided that was their destination for the night.

"Look here," Cass called. "There's stream-washed gravel way up here on the mountainside."

"You've got to be kidding. On a rocky mountainside?" Scotty left the mules and walked into the wash. It was two hundred feet in width and resembled the deep cut road builders sometimes make. Sure enough, the gravel was round and smooth.

"How can this be? There's isn't a stream or river within miles large enough to have caused this!"

"Maybe so," Cass said. "Not now, at least. But I know stream-washed gravel when I see it."

Chapter Two

✦

Discovery

Scotty examined the gravel, inspecting pieces of rounded quartz with his magnifying glass, then pulled a shovel from one of the mule packs and began to dig. Two feet down, he knelt and began sifting the sand and gravel through his fingers.

Suddenly Scotty whooped and held one hand overhead.

"By God, Cass. Here's a nugget!"

"If you're kidding me, you're going to both cook supper and do the dishes," Cass said dryly, picking up the birds and walking to where Scotty stood smiling broadly.

"So it is. And a beauty too." Cass hefted the heart-shaped nugget in his hand. "Rough. Hasn't came far. Make you a nice stick pin." He peered up the mountain as if expecting to see the mother lode protruding from nearby bedrock. An overhanging snow bank still covered the curious gully half a mile up its length.

"Here's another. Laced with quartz. Cass, I believe we've found something good. Both men went to work with their shovels. Four feet down they struck solid bedrock. This was doubly exciting. They were used to sinking shafts 20 to 50 feet deep to reach bedrock. Scraping out the cracks in the bedrock with hunting knives and spoons they picked out an ounce of coarse gold with their fingers. The price of gold was $17.00. They were tremendously excited. They put the gold in a spent cartridge.

The mules had wandered on down the slope in search of food. During mid-summer, darkness lasted but a few hours at this latitude. They worked until hunger caused them to stop.

40

"Oh, for some water to pan this sand with," Cass said. "I'm going to carry a pan down to the lake."

"We'd better make camp. I'm starved." Leading the mules, Scotty made his way down the mountainside to the lakeshore. Jabbering excitedly, they pitched camp. While Scotty cooked the birds with rice and gravy in the Dutch oven, Cass gathered wood and washed the pan of gravel. He returned to camp and handed the pan to Scotty. Scotty tipped the pan into the firelight, then whistled. A teaspoon full of yellow gold glistened in the pan. They'd made $32.00 in only a few hours!

"Whoopee!" Scotty shouted. Ignoring the hordes of mosquitos, grabbing Cass by the shoulders they danced around the fire, shouting and singing like men possessed. Which they surely were, by demon gold.

"We're gonna be rich. We're gonna be gold kings," Cass sang in his Irish tenor.

Too excited to sleep, they sat by the fire, smoked and talked, wondering how gold could have been deposited high on a mountainside. They considered the extent of the gold-bearing gravel. How far up the dry creek bed did it reach? How far down?

Across the lake a wolf howled, "AAAAOOOoooooooo!" From afar another answered. A common loon called to its mate on the lake. The last rays of the setting sun struck the snow-covered mountain peaks in the distance, turning them red.

"Who knows what the country looked like thousands, maybe millions of years ago. At one time I'll bet the glacier we noticed from the top of the pass reached here. Probably created this lake and this U-shaped basin. The exposed bedrock round here is smooth, as if it has been scraped by ice. Perhaps the ice retreated, leaving this stream bed high and dry." [2]

---

[2] *During the Klondike Gold Rush of 1897-98, experienced miners with claims on Bonanza Creek, below and above Discovery, scoffed when desperate prospectors climbed what's now called Gold Hill and staked "hillside" claims. The "hillside" claims turned out to be some of the richest ground in the Klondike, and are still being mined today. Mountains of loose, broken white quartz are still much in evidence. What is now considered a hill, is believed to have once been the stream bed of a huge, prehistoric river 1000 times larger than the present Yukon.*

"Maybe. I can hardly wait for daylight."

"We're gonna be rich, Scotty."

"Couldn't have happened to two nicer guys."

"Or more needy."

Daylight found the men back at the strike. They worked all day and added several ounces of coarse gold, nuggets, and gold-laced quartz to their pokes. Excited, they didn't take time to eat properly, wash clothes or take care of themselves. Each day was much the same as the previous, up early, a quick breakfast of meat, mush, sourdough biscuits or hotcakes, then up to the mine to dig trenches across the stream bed, sampling and sifting for nuggets. They worked as long as their backs would stand the labor, then stumbled down, panned the gravel they'd brought, ate a quick dinner and fell into bed.

They'd never heard of such rich placer deposits. They took special delight in the "picture rock", chunks of smooth, white quartz, some the size of walnuts, laced with pure, yellow gold. They kept the picture rock separate from the pure gold.

They began taking the mules to the mine, filling the panniers with gravel, then packing it down to the lake at quitting time to run through their small, knock-down portable rocker. They rejoiced at the amount of coarse gold they found, knowing it had not traveled far. Somewhere nearby was probably rich lode gold. They longed for water to sit up a rocker at the mine, but none was available.

They killed caribou or sheep for meat, jerking, drying and smoking some so it would keep in the hot weather. They wrapped meat in canvas to keep off flies, then hung it high in a tree some distance from camp in case a bear happened by. Grizzlies were frequently seen on the nearby slopes, feeding upon lush vegetation. Pieces of caribou hide were sewn into sturdy pokes for the gold.

"Scotty, it's too bad we haven't time to explore this area. There may be more gold-bearing streams. It would be nice to sample the surrounding country."

"That's true. But it's nicer to fill these pokes."

One day, several weeks after the initial strike, they noticed that the nights were cooler and the dwarf arctic birch, bearberry, wild rose, thistle and huckleberry, especially at higher elevations, had already turned brown, red and gold.

They discussed whether or not they should stake their claims. As discoverers in a new territory, they were entitled to one claim each, plus a Discoverer's Claim. Assured they were so far from civilization no one would be coming by anyway they decided against staking.

One day they started for camp from the mine leading both mules loaded with gravel. Suddenly the mules stopped, brayed, peered towards camp and refused to continue.

"Damn grizzly in camp, I'll bet," Cass growled. "After our meat supply." Leaving Scotty and the mules behind, Cass took his rifle and cautiously approached camp through the surrounding birch trees.

The bear was gone, but the tent was ripped in several places. Their grub boxes were smashed and most of the food missing or scattered in the dirt. The bear had gotten into their brown sugar, used to make syrup, and scattered their flour. Pawing through the mess, Cass discovered the bear had bitten into their compass, releasing the fluid, destroying it completely.

"Come on down. The bear's gone," Cass yelled. It took a lot of coaxing to get the mules into camp. They blew and brayed their dislike for the odor of grizzly. Cass held up the ruined compass. "I hope we have a good sense of direction when we head out," Cass said. Scotty looked at the compass and swore.

Aware of the destructiveness of bears, they'd cached a small reserve portion of their grub supply, flour, beans, rice, powered milk, coffee and dried fruit high in a nearby tree. This was no assurance it was secure, because black bears climb trees, while grizzlies seldom do. Cass checked the cache and reported it was still safe.

The bear attack, loss of the precious compass and signs of autumn, forced a sobering realization. Now short of food, they realized they must quit the country and start back. The next day they hit a richer pocket than before, with nuggets galore. Who could stop work under such conditions?

Like many a miner, they let greed overcome good judgement.

They also misjudged the severity of northern sub-arctic fall weather, that can be warm, even hot, one day, and a blizzard the next. They were located at about 4,000 feet in elevation, where snow can occur any month of the year, and periods of winter weather can arrive anytime after mid-August.

They had kept a calendar by entering the days in their journal. But the mine had been so exciting they had not made a single entry since the strike, and had lost track of time. They argued over whether it was late August or early September.

Even more disturbing was the condition of the mules. They had worked them unmercifully these past weeks, and only let one at a time loose at night. The nearby forage was used up, and the animals didn't receive as much nourishment as they required. Mosquitos and flies drove the animals mad. They rubbed tallow around their eyes, but the animals were suffering. Each night they'd stake one in a different location, but new patches of feed near camp were scarce. They hated to spend much time taking the animals to more distant places for the night. They were also afraid a bear might kill the mules.

Working long hours doing heavy work, both men lost considerable weight. And they ate a lot of meat, that meant Cass had to take time off for hunting frequently.

One morning they awoke to a tremendous display of Northern Lights flashing blue, green and amber in the northern sky. When Cass went to the lake for water, he had to break skim ice. Flocks of Canada geese flew south every day. Neither said much about the rapid changes in weather, although they recognized what such changes meant. They hurried off to the mine.

By now they had 12 large pokes of gold, each weighing about 80 ounces! A fortune in those days, close to $17,000.00, after only a few weeks of work.

Chapter Three

✦

Tragedy Strikes

One morning Scotty returned to camp with only one mule. Jake, the oldest, poorest animal had died during the night. With this sobering news, they decided they'd clean up the rich pocket, then leave. This meant they'd also have to carry heavier packs than expected. They'd leave the stove, tools and everything possible behind, and live off the country. They skinned the mule and used the hide for much needed repairs to their equipment and packs.

The sow grizzly and cubs quickly claimed the mule carcass and stayed with it until the flesh was gone. Cass intended to shoot the bears, then decided that would only pile up more meat which would attract more bears. Having the grizzlies living close by was uncomfortable.

The rich pocket continued to pay. Cass discovered the largest nugget either had ever seen, the size of a hazel nut. Now that they had only one mule, they also began backpacking a load of gravel to the lake at quitting time.

One dark night, they awoke to find dry snow blowing onto their faces through a hole in the tent made by the bear. "Only a squall," Scotty mumbled sleepily. "Early fall storm. Be over by morning."

By daylight it was snowing hard. The storm kept up all day. The men stayed in bed resting. They were completely worn out. By evening a foot of snow covered the ground and the storm had developed into a raging blizzard. They retrieved their cache of food, brought Jessie into the tent and prepared to leave as soon as the snow stopped.

Another day passed with no letup in the storm. The north wind howled and the lake froze over. Unprepared for such weather, they spent the day sewing crude mittens and caps out of caribou and sheep hide.

"This can't last," Scotty predicted. "It'll pass, and we'll have several weeks of Indian summer."

Cass made a trip to the mine to look for the tools. He returned to report drifting snow had covered the diggings. "Snow's lots deeper up there. We've gotta get outta here fast!"

The snow stopped, but the sky remained overcast. Hurriedly packing, hiding the stove and other abandoned camp goods away from the lake in a clump of birch, they loaded Jessie and their packs and headed for Caribou Pass.

The snow quickly grew deeper and deeper as they climbed. Soon it was up to their waists. Jessie stopped, panting and wheezing. Despite their best coaxing and threatening, Jessie refused to continue. Both men were already worn out. They looked at each other with consternation.

"We're not going to make it over Caribou Pass," Scotty sighed.

"We waited too long," Cass said. "We got too greedy."

Except for Caribou Pass, over which they'd came, a high, jagged mountain range, across which neither a heavily loaded man nor beast could climb, effectively blocked their route towards Dease Lake.

"If we follow this side of the range we'll find a place to cross at a lower elevation," Scotty said.

"Remember the day I climbed that high peak yonder looking for a sheep? I think I could see into the Tuya Valley to the southwest. We could just follow the river to Telegraph Creek. I forgot to mention it."

"Good idea. Problem is, Telegraph Creek is probably three times as far as Dease Lake."

"Well, we haven't anything better to do." [3]

---

[3] *What they didn't realize, was that on their way into the country, they had crossed the upper Tuya without knowing, and continued on northwest. Actually the watershed Cass thought was the Tuya was probably the Nahlin, that flows into the Taku. The Tuya River, from its source to where it joins the Stikine, on a southerly course, is about 80 miles long.*

They returned to camp, put up the tent, built a campfire and spent the night. They didn't say much, but each was wondering what they had gotten themselves into. Early the next day they started on their new course, following along the mountainside, holding their elevation, looking for a pass. It was slow, rough going, with many steep ravines to cross. A few miles a day was all they could cover. For three days they followed the range without finding a pass. A heavy cloud layer hovered around the peaks, effectively blocking the sun, their only method of telling directions.

On the fourth day, Scotty was leading Jessie across a rockslide along the mountainside above a cliff that dropped off into a deep valley. The wind had blown most of the snow off the ground. Cass, as usual, was ahead, scouting the best route.

Suddenly Scotty stumbled into a massive underground yellow jacket nest. Before he could lead the terrified mule away, Jessie stamped madly over the nest. An angry swarm of bees erupted and attack both Jessie and Scotty. Stung repeatedly about the face, Scotty dropped the lead rope and covered his eyes with his hands, fighting off the insects. Jessie, let out a snort and, eyes covered with bees, charged blindly down the mountain!

"Cass. Help. Yellow jackets!" Scotty's face was already going numb.

"Where's Jessie?" Cass yelled, throwing off his pack and scooting downhill towards Scotty.

"Don't know. I'm stung bad."

Cass circled around the yellow jacket's nest, slid down and peered over the cliff. "Jessie's lodged upside down against a spruce tree. Right on the brink of a sheer drop off. Stupid mule!"

"That's just great! Damn yellow jackets did a number on me. My left eye's swelling shut," Scotty said, shedding his pack. "Hurts like hell!"

"Jessie's badly hurt, or dead! His head's flopping back and forth and his hooves are pawing the air," Cass yelled.

"Oh! My God. The pokes!" Scotty groaned. Dizzily, he laid back against the hillside.

"One pack tore loose from its lashings, slipped out from under the tent, and is dangling down from the saddle over the cliff. The other pack's squashed beneath his back. Jessie's dead. Lord, Lord. What are we going to do?"

"Recover the gold. What else? But I can't help. My eyes are streaming tears and my nose is numb. I feel like I'm going to faint."

"You stay up there where it's safe. We've got enough trouble without you falling over the cliff too."

Cass retrieved some rope and managed to unload one pack, dragging the heavy pokes and supplies uphill to the bench. The other pack, containing five pokes of gold, their Dutch oven and some of their remaining grub supplies, was beneath the dead mule. If he dislodged Jessie, mule and pack would both tumble down the cliff.

"We've got to retrieve that gold. Otherwise, we'll have to circle around those cliffs, climb down into that canyon and carry it back up," Cass growled.

"If they drop they'll probably break open and scatter gold all over the cliff." Scotty groaned.

Tying the mule's packsaddle to the tree, Cass took the axe and began chopping off the dead mule 's hind quarters. Blood and stomach contents flew onto his face and saturated his pants. A terrible stench filled the air. Finally, with a final blow that severed the backbone, the mule's rear end slid over the cliff and tumbled out of sight into the canyon with a thud. Cass cut the cinch and the front quarters slipped out of the tied off pack saddle and disappeared.

"It was the Dutch oven on top of the pack under the tent that broke his back," Cass yelled up to Scotty. " I salvaged the gold and everything except the pack saddle."

"Poor devil."

"Poor devil, indeed. I think Jessie committed suicide. I knew the mules were terrified of yellow jackets, but didn't think Jessie would do that. After we back pack this gold out, we may wish it had been us that died, cause we're surely going to have broken backs too."

"Oh, hell," Scotty said. "I can't see. Snot is running out of my nose and my eyes are streaming tears. But complaining ain't going to do no good. Let's get on with it. Shit! Just when everything was looking so rosy."

Cass led Scotty by the hand to a safe place where he could be comfortable while he lugged their belongings to a level pocket at the base of a huge rock slide where there was a small depression and plenty of snow for water. He built a fire, pitched the tent, helped Scotty to camp and laid him on the blankets.

"You gonna be all right?" Cass questioned.

"I don't know. I've been stung before but those little bastards were especially lethal." Scotty groaned. "I'm sick as hell."

Cass gave a nervous laugh.

"I'll be damned if I see anything funny," Scotty growled.

"Look at that bloody pile of gold. The heaviest damn stuff in the world, and we've got to lug it out on our backs!"

"That's funny? You have a queer sense of humor today. We've been in tough spots before, but I've never seen you break up about it."

"Yeah. We have. We always figured a way out. This time it's different. We're rich. But I'll be damned if it isn't funny. One day we were rich and now, well, Partner, I can't see any easy way out."

"We'll make it, even without Jessie."

"How do you propose we are going to pack all this gold?"

"I'm more worried about something to eat. We can't eat gold."

"Old dead eye here will keep us in meat," Cass answered, petting his rifle fondly. "Never let you starve before, have I?"

Scotty slept fitfully because of the pain. At daylight Cass inquired how he was feeling. "Not good, but we have to get going. First we gotta get rid of that picture rock."

"Right. Lucky we kept it in separate pokes." Cass got up, built a fire and hung the tea can over the flames..

"How much you think the rest of the gold will weigh?"

"Sixty pounds. Maybe more."

"With the camping gear, about 65 or 70 pounds each."

"What'll we do with the quartz?"

"Bury it in the rock slide yonder. Come back for it in the spring."

They repacked, leaving everything they could, even Cass's prized 1851-model Navy Colt revolver, for which he had no more ammunition. They dug a hole beneath a prominent boulder in the rock slide and cached the gold-laced quartz and excess baggage. Scotty noticed Cass finger the revolver lovingly, pressing it against his lips, before he tossed it into the cache.

They took a close look at the surrounding country so they could find the cache again. Pack sacks bulging, they started out. They were used to carrying heavy loads on their backs, but this additional weight was plainly too much.

Twice they tried to cross the range. Both times they had to turn back because of deep snow and steep country. They had came a long ways southwest from the mine.

Positive they were cut off from Dease Lake, they had little choice but to head for the Tuya and Telegraph Creek, although they were unsure of where the Tuya River was. All they knew was if they kept going south they'd eventually find either the river, or the Moore Trail. By descending into the inviting valley in the distance they'd be going down hill and out of the snow. Once they got into the river valley, there would be game, or so they hoped.

The gray overcast continued. Frequent snow squalls scurried across the mountains, accompanied by a cold wind. Cursing because he didn't have his compass, Scotty relied upon his sense of direction.

Now that they had decided to follow what they thought was the Tuya River valley, there was no point in staying high, so they headed down. By nightfall they had left the deep snow behind and were in mixed pine and birch timber.

Scotty was the navigator and Cass the hunter. It had always been that way with the partners. Scotty's sense of direction was better than his partner's, but he had an uneasy feeling they were going the wrong way. He didn't mention the fact to Cass. Because of the persistent overcast sky, he couldn't confirm directions. They staggered on, the crude pack straps, reinforced with mule hide, cutting unmercifully into their skinny shoulders, stopping often to rest.

Two days later, the storm broke and the sky cleared. They were amazed to discover, that although they had been following the range above a river valley, they had been heading north east, directly opposite from the direction they wanted to go!

For a long time they sat cursing their bad luck, cursing the grizzly that had ruined their compass, the overcast, the mules, yellow jackets and the weight of gold.

"How could this have happened?" Cass growled.

"Obviously, the watershed we're following isn't the Tuya. In fact, it's probably not even a tributary of the Stikine. It's some other unknown damned river," Scotty said. "Running off towards who knows where. In other words, we're lost!" [4]

"Great! That's just great."

Scotty detected the irony in Cass' voice. "This is a first. We've never been lost before."

"Let's hope it isn't the last," Cass mumbled.

"We'll have to go back to where we cached the gold, then start out again."

"Why did nature have to make gold so heavy? Why couldn't it be light, like asbestos?" Cass grumbled. Hoisting their heavy pack sacks, they began retracing their steps of the past several days.

The route was uphill! They were soon back in deep snow. Every step was torture. They barely inched along, sweating, slipping and panting. It started snowing again, and the wind blew snow across their back trail. Darkness came and they were forced

---

[4] *The men were probably following the headwaters of the Jennings or Teslin Rivers in the Tuya Mountains, something they'd never have done if they had a compass.*

Averaging approximately 4000 feet in elevation, with mountains well over 6,000 feet elevation, the Plateau experiences extreme winter weather. Chilkoot Pass, slightly higher, not much farther north, for example, is notorious for its foul weather, has 9 or 10 months subject to winter weather and 20 to 50 feet of snow can accumulate.

to pitch their canvas shelter on the steep mountainside. There was no firewood. They spent a long, cold, miserable night huddled together under damp blankets, with only the canvas to shed snow and wind. They spent most of the night discussing alternate plans, deciding to cache most of the gold and proceed with lighter packs. When dawn arrived there was no place to cache anything where it could be found again. Wearily they loaded the heavy packs and began clawing up the mountain again. The only game tracks they'd seen had been headed down the mountain, except for several grizzly tracks, that were headed up into the deep snow where they preferred to den for the winter.

Three days later they reached "Dead Mule Cache." An entire week had been wasted. Starving, weary, discouraged, Cass took the rifle and axe, circled around the cliff and went down to where Jessie had fallen into the ravine. He hoped to chop out some frozen meat. As he approached the location, back in an alcove at the base of the cliff, he saw ravens take to the air. Creeping closer, he saw something brown move. The charge took Cass totally by surprise. He had assumed bears were all denned up for the winter. Instinctively Cass dropped the axe, thrust the 45-70 rifle out and pulled the trigger. The bear never flinched. Before he could reload the bear crashed into him, knocking him flying.

When he regained consciousness blood was running from a cut in his head. He peered around cautiously, thinking the bear was watching, but couldn't see any movement. Cass examined himself cautiously, expecting the worst. No bones were broken and the cut on his head was only a scratch. A lump was forming where his head had struck a rock, and his head ached. He found his rifle ten feet away in the brush. Jessie's carcass had been reduced to skin and bones. Cass didn't take time to look for blood or sign that he'd hit the bear, and began the long climb back to camp.

Scotty listened to Cass's story with astonishment. The sudden storm, losing both mules, getting lost and now the bear attack. Their good luck had suddenly turned bad. Cass vowed to shoot every grizzly on sight.

Obviously, they couldn't continue to carry so much weight. They split the pokes evenly and each decided how much he wanted to carry. The rest went into the cache under the rock.

"I wonder if we'll be able to find this again?" Cass said, peering around. "Let's build a cairn on top?"

Scotty shrugged. "So someone else might start probing around? We'll find it. Hell, there's a fortune left here."

The next day they felt like traveling again. With lighter packs they made better time, but it was still slow going, with knee-deep snow lying on steep ground. Finding fuel for a fire was a time-consuming task.

Eventually they crossed what they had been looking for, a natural pass south, into a new watershed. Ahead was another large, rolling basin, surrounded by mountains. Several long, narrow lakes were in the distance, water that had been trapped by the steps of the plateau.

"Ah!" Scotty said. "That has to be the Tuya."

They reached the first of the lakes. It was a quarter of a mile wide, but three miles long. They tested the thickness of the ice beneath the snow with their axe. It was too thin to support their weight. They grumbled every step, while forcing their way through willows and bogs still unfrozen beneath the snow, as they detoured around the lake.

This was only the first of a series of lakes that required long detours. Enough snow covered the thin ice to insulate it and prevent it from freezing thick enough to support their weight. After circling around one lake, they thought they would have good going, then they'd stumble upon another, test the ice, then resort to a miserable detour around. Another snow storm hit. The heavy loads, inadequate food and long, cold nights took their toll. They decided they were suffering the first signs of scurvy and began to drink spruce tea.

Strangely enough, a country that had teemed with game during the summer now seemed devoid of animals. They walked all day without seeing a track. Perhaps, they reasoned, the animals knew something they didn't; the beginning of an early, hard winter. They subsisted for several days on a grouse and one fat porcupine. Each night they set wire snares in rabbit runs, but rabbits were scarce also.

One morning their snares held a Canadian lynx. They skinned it and ate the meat. It was surprisingly good. They cut the fur into boot liners and sewed crude mittens.

One evening Cass propped his boots on sticks in front of the fire to dry while setting up the tarp shelter. Scotty was off gathering wood. Suddenly Cass yelled curses. Scotty rushed to the fire to find Cass examining his steaming, scorched boot.

"Damn boot fell into the fire," Cass grumbled.

"Ruined?"

"I don't think so. Scorched though."

When he put it on and started walking the following morning, the sole cracked in half! They wrapped mule hide around the sole.

The days were hard, but the long, long nights seemed endless. To keep from freezing, they slept together fully clothed under their blankets to conserve warmth. The canvas shelter did not keep out the wind. Keeping a fire going all night was often impossible.

"Such a damn country. Doesn't make sense," Scotty protested. "Water running every which way." Secretly, he feared they were still lost, but didn't mention the fact to Cass.

Wolves sometimes followed them, just out of range for a sure, killing shot. Their howls caused the hair on the men's necks to stiffen with fear.

To pass the long, cold night hours, they talked about their plans, how they intended to develop their mine. They decided the slope was steep enough they could rig up a cable tram to transport gravel to the lake. Loaded buckets would pull empties back to the diggings. For that they would need a mile of cable. Hauling cable on horses over the passes would be a formidable task. If the gravel was rich enough for them to have removed so much gold with only their fingers and a pan, what could it produce if they began regular placer mining operations?

They also spent hours talking about what they'd do after they became millionaires. Cass planned to move to the Santa Clara Valley in California, find a Spanish wife, buy valley land, hire workers, raise oranges and fruit, and become a gentleman farmer. Scotty thought he'd buy hotels, maybe in Victoria, a city that appeared to be thriving. He'd met a lady there that he liked. Maybe he'd ask her to marry. Such fantasies helped warm their cold bodies, helped distract from their dark, cruel surroundings. Eventually they'd drop off to sleep. Sometimes they had vivid, morbid dreams, of golden riches, of wolves snarling over their prone bodies, of freezing, starving and the unending trek they faced.

One morning before daybreak, as they sat wrapped in their filthy blankets watching the fire, with the Northern Lights flickering overhead, Cass said, "Last night I dreamed we went under. I looked down and saw both of our frozen skeletons scattered in the snow. Varmints had picked us clean. Gold dust was scattered all around. God, it was terrible."

Scotty shuddered, and took his time to answer. "We've waited for years to get rich. Now that we are, I don't plan on dying."

"Yeah. But we ain't rich until we get it to the bank." There was no doubt about his discouragement.

"Don't give up, Cass. If you do, look how far I'd have to come back for your share of the gold."

"That was an unkind thing to say. I ain't gonna let you spend my gold. I'll keep going, even if I have to crawl."

The next morning, with the temperature far below freezing, they were crossing what they thought was a snow-covered beaver pond or shallow muskeg. They neglected to test with the axe to see if the ice was thick enough to support their weight. Patches of brush protruded above the snow, as if it was only a shallow swamp.

Suddenly Cass, in the lead, carrying the shotgun, crashed through the ice. The heavy pack drove Cass under water. He dropped the gun and grabbed the edge of the ice, pulling his head above water.

"Quick, get me outta here, " he screamed, spouting water..

Scotty, ten yards behind, threw off his pack and cautiously approached the jagged hole in the ice. Suddenly ice began to crack under his weight. Terrified, Scotty flung himself prone and rolled to safety.

"I can't help. I'll break through too," Scotty yelled. "I'll get a pole." Fortunately, he carried the axe and woods were nearby.

Scotty chopped down a pine tree 20 feet high, dragged it to near where Cass clung desperately to the ice and shoved the butt across the hole.

"I'm numb. I'm going down."

"No you're not. Don't give up!"

Cass clung to the pole with both hands. "I can't pull myself out with this dam pack dragging me down. You'll have to help. I can't hold on much longer."

"Throw off the pack, Cass"

"No! My gold. I can't. If I let go it'll sink."

"Better to lose the gold than die. Work your arms out of the straps one at a time."

Scotty could see Cass struggling with the pack straps. "I can't. Help me."

Scotty worked his way out the pole until he was close to Cass. Taking out his knife, he tried to reach under the water and cut the pack straps.

"No. That's my GOLD!" Cass screamed.

"DON'T BE A DAMN FOOL! I'll give you half of mine. We can always go back and get more gold."

"Get me out, please!" Cass pleaded.

Scotty reached under the icy water, grabbed the pack straps and heaved. He kept losing his balance and almost fell in. Despite his best efforts he couldn't lift the heavy weight.

"If I had two poles, maybe I could get you out."

"Well. Get another, then."

"Can you hold on?"

"A minute, maybe."

Scotty ran into the woods and cut another pine. With poles on both sides he slid the pack off Cass's back, then hauled him out.

Cass was too numb to walk. Scotty skidded him ashore. By the time he reached shore, Cass's clothing were frozen stiff! Unable to unbutton his coat, Scotty started to slice the clothing off with his knife, then remembered they didn't have enough thread to sew them back together again.

Luckily there was a supply of dead wood nearby. Wrapping Cass's bare head in his dry coat and blanket, Scotty built a roaring fire.

Cass was moaning, shivering and shaking uncontrollably. "We've got to thaw your clothes enough so we can get them off to dry," Scotty growled. "Shit! Shit." Damn this cold."

He hung the tea pot over the flames and began rolling Cass back and forth by the fire. Cass's teeth chattered and he groaned with pain, complaining his back felt broke. Finally the wet clothing thawed enough to remove. He wrapped Cass in their dry blanket and sat him by the fire while he pitched the shelter. There would be no traveling for the rest of that day.

While he dried Cass's clothing they drank scalding cups of tea. Drying Cass's clothes, blanket and boots required all day. Cass was strangely quiet. He kept mumbling, "Luck's all used up. We ain't going to make it, Scotty!"

"Hey, partner, we had some good and some bad luck. We're going to be okay. It could have been worse. We could have both fell through the ice." Scotty heated stones to place at their feet beneath the blankets, then cuddled against his partner's shivering body in an attempt to warm him.

"That was a bloody brave thing you done for me, Scotty," Cass mumbled during the night.

"You would've done the same for me. At least you smell better."

"If we'd have both went in......"

"But we didn't."

"Well, anyway, I owe you my life."

"Cut the bullshit. What else could I have done? Sit on the bloody shore and watch you drown? And lose all that gold too."

"Damn the gold. It's going to be the death of us yet," Cass gritted.

"You've always had a positive attitude. Why change now?"

"Because my feet and my hands and my balls feel frozen and my back feels like it's broken, that's why."

"Remember Francine? Maybe that'll warm you up," Scotty said.

When it came time to leave camp the following morning Cass could hardly move. He complained that his back was out of place. His feet and legs ached so bad he couldn't stand. They took the day off. The shotgun was now on the bottom of the lake. Scotty searched for it with a fishhook, but gave up, took the rifle and went hunting. He saw a snowshoe rabbit, but didn't want to waste a bullet on it. They ate a little rice and rested. The snares remained empty.

The next morning Cass screamed with pain when Scotty helped him shoulder his pack. Scotty took as much of his partner's load as he could.

After the dunking, three miles was all Cass could cover in a day and every step was torture. His broken shoe leaked and his right foot was constantly wet and cold. Their food supply was nearly exhausted. Both were out of tobacco. Worse yet, their match supply was getting low. Scotty used a gallon can, punched holes in the sides for ventilation, and began carrying live coals.

One evening Scotty was in the lead, carrying the rifle. A cow moose was feeding in the willows. Throwing his pack, Scotty made a long, circular stalk until the moose was upwind, then sneaked in and killed the animal with one shot.

"Good shot," Cass yelled. "I'm proud of you." Scotty cut out the back straps and liver. They made camp 100 yards away and roasted strips of loins and fat over the fire. Before the meat was cooked, they gobbled it down. Famished, they gorged themselves.

The rich food made them sick and they writhed with pain and vomited the meat. Within an hour they ate again. It took several attempts before they held the food down. Scotty put fat meat and rice into their one kettle and let it simmer to make broth. Strips of bloody liver, toasted over the coals, were especially nourishing.

During the night the men awoke to loud noises from the scene of the kill. "Wolves," Scotty said, getting out of the blankets and adding wood to the fire. Glowing eyes stared out of the nearby brush. Scotty aimed between the eyes and pulled the trigger. The eyes disappeared. There was no sleep the rest of the night for Scotty. Cass slept fitfully .

At daylight Scotty found a dead wolf twenty yards from the fire. The moose carcass had been partly devoured. Several wolves, gorged with meat, were curled up in nearby willows. Scotty shot at one but missed. The wolves slunk off.

"Must have been a big pack," Scotty said, shuddering, thinking of what might happen if they decided to attack. He skinned the wolf, divided the hide and made warm caps and mittens. They rubbed moose tallow on their boots.

They stayed in camp that day. Cass remained in his blankets. Scotty worked all day on a moose hide overshoe for Cass's broken boot. That night wolves returned to the kill, fighting and howling.

The rest and meat revived them enough they continued on. The Tuya River or the Moore Trail had to be near now.

The weather turned to mixed rain and snow. Scotty wondered if they were completely lost. Huddled under the tarp, in front of a smoky fire, they were constantly wet, cold and miserable. Their footwear was inadequate for such conditions and their feet were constantly wet. Their legs cramped at night until they couldn't sleep.

A week after leaving the site of the break through in the ice, they climbed a low divide. Yet another river lay to the south, but it wasn't large enough to be the Stikine. "Gotta be the Tuya," Scotty said. The river was running ice, but wasn't frozen. They camped beside the river for two days to rest. It was a pleasant location, with a big rock to reflect the campfire, and a view across the river.

Mink, otter, marten and snowshoe rabbit sign were plentiful. Scotty set rabbit snares. It had been six weeks, they thought, since they'd left the mine.

Scotty was worried about Cass' health after he'd gone through the ice. He'd developed a terrible cough. With an injured back every step was painful. Scotty also noticed Cass' feet smelled rotten and there were specks of blood in his spit.

The rabbit snares yielded two snowshoe rabbits. They roasted one for dinner and kept the other for breakfast.

When it came time to break camp, Cass refused to leave.

"You go ahead. See if you can find help."

Scotty considered this. "If I don't?"

"I'll be all right. Just leave me the snares and help me get in a wood supply. Lean willows against the rock and put a piece of canvas over it."

"It's probably mid-October. Winter, real winter, might set in anytime. I might not be able to return, even if I did locate help."

"It's too painful to travel, Scotty. I ain't no quitter. You know that. Alone you could make ten miles a day, or more. I can't go even three. We'll both starve, or freeze to death. Besides, along a river like this, with all these fur-bearing animals, must be Indians living here somewhere. Just keep going down until you find them. Maybe you can hire them to come back with dog sleds. If we offer them enough gold, maybe they'll haul us both out of here."

"Wouldn't that be nice. Maybe one of their women would sit between us on the sled to keep us warm." Scotty laughed.

Cass found no humor in the thought."There's no sense of both of us dying."

Scotty was at a loss of what to do. Cass's heavy, rasping breathing was proof that his lungs were congested.

Scotty recognized merit in Cass' plan. But what if he didn't find help? He would be unable to return and Cass would surely starve or die of exposure.

It was noon before Scotty made a painful decision."I guess I'll look for help," he said, starting to pack his gear.

Cass nodded. They divided the blankets and the tarp. Scotty carried in a big supply of wood, fixed the shelter as best he could, then put on his pack. "I'm leaving you the rifle," he said.

"No, you take it. I couldn't hunt anyway. The snares will keep me from starving. 'Sides, we don't know if these Natives are hostile or not."

"A moose might come through camp."

"If I shot it, I'd have more wolves for company."Cass struggled to his feet. "Partner, you take care of yourself." He hugged Scotty close for a long time, then turned his back to hide his face and held his hands out to the fire.

Scotty walked slowly away. When he turned to look back, Cass was still standing hunched over like he'd left him. Scotty walked half a mile, then sank down in the snow and cried. Without Cass, he didn't have much to live for. He turned around and returned to the fire.

"What did you forget?" Cass said. His face betrayed his feelings.

"You," Scotty said. He flung down his pack, took the axe and looked Cass square in the eye. "We're sticking together."

"Don't be a bloody fool. There's no reason why we should both die."

"I've an idea. I used to watch those Indians moving camp. I'm going to drag you for a spell."

Scotty cut a supply of limber willows and tossed them near the fire, instructing Cass to thaw them and strip off some bark. He cut two stout lodgepole pine about ten feet long.

"What are you making?"

"A *travois* to drag your lazy ass on. Now, pitch in and help."

The heated willows were woven into a basket, then lashed between the poles with bark. They used a piece of moose hide as a tow strap around Scotty's shoulders. After it was finished, Cass laid down on the litter and Scotty dragged him around through the snow on a practice run. It worked perfectly. They even placed both packs on the lower ends. The next morning they were on their way.

After a while Cass called out. "I'm glad you thought of this, partner."

"I get five dollars a day for this. Hell, a tenderfoot kid like you wouldn't have lasted two more days without me to take care of you," Scotty retorted. He was two years older than Cass, and never let him forget it.

The litter worked well until they had to go uphill, or through thickets of timber. Then Cass had to walk. It hurt Scotty to watch him hobble along, but Cass never complained. They cut forked branches for crutches. Progress was painfully slow, but at least they were together.

The river was low so sometimes they traveled snow-covered gravel bars and made good time. When they had to take to the brush around dangerous ice Scotty quickly tired.

One afternoon they noticed an old axe blaze on a birch tree, the first sign of man they'd seen in over three months. Scotty found a rusty marten trap hanging nearby. "Someone's trapping ground," Scotty said, taking the trap. "We'll catch rabbits with this," putting the trap on the sled.

The next day they were passing through a stand of willows when they saw a fresh moccasin print and dog tracks in the snow. "If we find an Indian camp, we'll cache most of the gold before we go in."

"Won't be easy. Ground frozen like it is."

"I know. But to have this much gold! There's no way we could hide the fact from them."

"True. True. What do you think these local Indians are like?"

"I expect they're like Indians, and whites for that matter, everywhere. Some are friendly, some hostile. Like they were in the Fraser and Cariboo, I suppose."

Yard by yard, mile by mile, encouraged by the signs of man, Scotty labored on through the wilderness, the travois poles making two furrows through the snow.

Chapter Four

✦

With the Tahltans

They were looking for a place to camp that evening, rejecting any spot where firewood wasn't readily available, when suddenly they heard dogs bark. An Indian, carrying a canvas pack on his back and leading four wild-looking dogs loaded with packs, came around a clump of brush fifty yards away. Walking ahead was a small black, white and tan Tahltan bear dog with pointed, erect ears. The pack dogs growled. Startled, the Indian raised his musket and pointed it at Scotty.

"Tillicum! Friend!" Scotty shouted, dropping his burden and holding his hands in the air to show he wasn't armed. Cass kept his rifle beneath the blankets.

"Hello. You speak English?"

The Indian lowered his musket, nodded and looked at them suspiciously. "Some." His hair was cut collar-length, his face smooth. He wore a fur cap, dark woolen trading post clothing and a dirty, red Hudson's Bay blanket, with a hole cut for his head, over his shoulders. He had a wild, savage look. "*Tak-ke-yehk*," he hissed, regarding the strangers suspiciously. Their clothing were rags, their hair and beards long, matted and unkempt and they wore strange-looking fur caps.

"What river is this?"

"Thought you were earth spirits! *Tak-ke-yehk*! Tuya River."

"You live near here?"

The man nodded and pointed down river. "Little ways. What's matter him?" he said, pointing at Cass.

"Bad feet. White man dumb. Fell through ice," Cass admitted.

The Indian thought about this, then admitted, " Me fall through ice too. Sometimes."

"What's your name?"

"Charlie."

Scotty introduced himself and Cass.

"What you do here?"

"Prospecting. From the high country up there," Scotty said, pointing. One moon hard travel. Much snow. Looking for Moore Trail. Telegraph Creek."

The Indian shook his head in amazement. " Up there? Long ways," he said with awe, glancing at their boots.

"Your camp. Can we find it if we keep going down the river?"

The Indian shrugged, thought for a moment, then motioned them to follow.

"Camp not far," he said.

"This your trap? I found it up the river a ways. Was going to try and catch something to eat with it. We're starving. Grub all gone."

Charlie took the trap without speaking. They followed a well-traveled trail, and quickly fell behind.

"Well, so much for your idea about caching the gold," Cass said.

"We'll have to make the best of it."

The camp consisted of three crude log huts built into the side of a clay bank a quarter of a mile up the mouth of a small stream flowing into the river. The back half of the cabins were completely covered with earth, and the exposed roof was covered by a thick layer of sod. Brush grew out of the sod, indicating the cabins were old. Rusty stovepipes jutted from the roofs of each cabin, but wood smoke only came from one. The cabins had no windows and only one door at the front. A moose hide served as a door.

A dozen wild-looking dogs were chained to trees. They began barking and straining at their chains until Charlie silenced them with a club and terse threats. A dog sled was propped against one hut. A crude cache had been built between two trees. Tin was nailed around the trees to keep animals from climbing. Several pair of snow shoes and dog harness hung from the cache.

The moose hide door opened slightly. Three faces stared out, surprised to see visitors, especially white strangers.

Charlie unloaded his dogs, tossed the packs onto the cache, then pointed.

"My house," Charlie said, motioning them to enter. The smell of cooking meat filled the warm interior of the cabin. The odor caused the miner's stomachs to rumble painfully. A candle sat in a tin can on a shelf above a hand-made table. A huge cast iron Dutch oven bubbled on the sheet metal stove. Two children, a boy and girl, about six years old, shrank back into the shadows, watching intently. Several blocks of wood served as stools. In the back end of the cabin were two bunks made of poles and covered with evergreen boughs, dry grass and thick, Four-Point Hudson Bay blankets.

Several beaver, mink, ermine and fox hides were propped against the wall to dry on stretcher boards.

The woman was about 30, rather pretty, with Oriental features definitely lighter than most Indians. She wore heavy woolen skirts and a calico shirt. Her feet were encased in knee-length beaded moosehide moccasins. Long braids of black hair hung over each shoulder to her waist.

Charlie spoke to his wife in their native tongue. She filled tin plates to the brim with boiled moose meat and gave one to each man. They ate silently, drinking the juice, asking for more. The children remained by the bunks, their black eyes fastened upon the strangers.

"Very good. Wife good cook," Cass offered. " We pay."
Charlie shook his head no. " I kill big moose. Plenty meat."
"You stay here all winter?"
"Trapping camp. We go to Tahltan before breakup."
"You Tahltan?"
"Me Tahltan. Wife Casca."
" Who lives in the other cabins?"
"Uncle. Brother-in-law. Wife's sister. Another Tahltan man. They come with new sled sometime. Maybe one month."

Casca Indian woman gathering wood on snowshoes in the Cassiar.

"What's your wife's name?"

"Lenora."

"She speak English?"

"Some."

"Well, Charlie," Scotty said, "as you can see, Cass is unable to walk. He hurt his back when he fell though the ice, and his feet

66

are bad. Would you take him to Telegraph Creek on your sled? We'll pay, of course."

Charlie looked startled, as if the question caught him by surprise. He shook his head no.

"Why not? We'll pay plenty gold."

Charlie looked at their ragged, dirty clothing, then at their heavy packs, and again shook his head no.

"Why not?"

"Not time."

"You do not have time to take him?"

"Not time to use sled."

"Oh, there's not enough snow?"

"Not enough ice."

"Oh, the river must freeze solid before you can travel downriver with a sled, is that right?"

Charlie nodded.

"So, you came up here with pack dogs?"

Charlie nodded yes. "Weather good then. Bad now."

"Well, after the river freezes, will you take him?"

"Cannot leave Lenora and children! Long way. Dangerous ice. Much trouble."

"Cass needs a doctor. We'll pay plenty."

"No doctor Telegraph."

"Doctor at Fort Wrangell?"

"Tlingit doctor, maybe. No white. River boat gone for winter. Breakup time, river boat come. Long time away in spring."

"I see." Scotty was stumped. He looked at Cass.

"Lenora, make tea," Charlie commanded sharply. He resented how she watched the strangers. Lenora dumped a palm full of tea in a simmering lard can of boiling water on the back of the stove. She remained silent, smiling, her back to the fire, intently watching every move the strangers made.

"Feed dogs," Charlie said, pulling on his coat, motioning for the men to follow. He lighted a candle lantern made from a gallon can. Scotty and Cass followed Charlie outside. Snow drifted silently through the pine boughs. Charlie placed the candle on a block of wood, pulled two dog packs off the cache and dumped frozen meat onto a chopping block. The dogs barked excitedly and lunged against the ends of their chains. Charlie chopped the frozen meat into portions with the axe, throwing one portion to each dog.

Back inside, the fragrance of fresh tea filled the hut. Lenora filled four empty cans. Charlie dumped heaping tea-spoons of sugar into his tea, then offered the sugar to his guests.

Cass and Scotty had not tasted tea or sugar for over a month. They were starved for sweets. "Good," Scotty said, smiling. "No tea or coffee for long, long time." After they finished the tea Charlie threw a moosehide on the dirt floor. "You sleep here," he said. Charlie, Lenora and the children went to their bunks and covered themselves with blankets.

Cass and Scotty rolled into their blankets and blew out the candle. It was the first time they'd slept warm in weeks.

At daylight Cass and Scotty went outside to the toilet, a canvas windbreak between two trees. "Think he knows why these packs are so heavy?" Cass asked.

"Probably. We offered to pay in gold didn't we. And we do not appear wealthy, do we?"

"What should we do?"

"See if he will let you stay here until I can either come back for you, or until there's enough ice they can freight you out."

"And you?"

"If they'll let you stay, I'm going on."

Cass nodded. "My feet are getting worse."

"I'm sorry, Cass. I don't know what else to do. I'll stay here today and rest up. If the snow stops I'll leave tomorrow."

But the snow didn't stop. A blizzard blew down the river. The wind moaned through the pines. The men stayed inside out of the storm. Charley made new dog harness while Lenore carefully fleshed several pelts. The children played with the Tahltan bear dog.[5]

Scotty asked Charlie to draw him a map, showing their location and Telegraph Creek. Charlie drew a rough sketch on a piece of white moose hide.

"How far to Telegraph Creek?" Scotty asked.

"With sled, on river, this many days." Charlie held up five fingers. "Through brush with dog packs, this many days." He held up all ten fingers. "Many bad places. Much steep. Many cliffs."

"Charlie, Cass can't walk. If we paid you two dollars a day in gold, could he stay here until I can return for him, or until someone can sled him out?"

Charlie and Lenora talked this over in their own language for a long, long time, gesturing excitedly. Two dollars a day was a fabulous amount. Finally, Charlie said he could stay in one of the other cabins. They agreed to supply food and wood.

Lenora fed them moose stew cooked with rice and dried potatoes. By morning the snow had stopped. Cass hobbled outside on his crutches to say goodbye.

"We're lucky they're honest. Not savages. They're not happy about having you stay, but the money convinced them. Try getting them to sled you to Telegraph Creek as soon as possible. I'm hoping to hire someone to sled me down the river to Fort Wrangell. We'll meet in the spring at Dease Lake, right after breakup. I'll arrange to have a big outfit shipped up, horses and all. We'll hire some help and give that mine hell."

"Sounds good, partner. I'll be there with bells on," Cass said, but he didn't sound very convincing.

"What do you intend to do with your gold?"

---

[5] *The Tahltan bear dog was not only unique to northern British Columbia, but, except for breeds used by Eskimo, was aboriginal to North America. The first white man to write about these little dogs was the explorer Samuel Black, who ventured into the headwaters of the Stikine River as early as 1824. Similar to beagles, they were trained to search out bears, then dart about in front of the bruins until the hunter arrived with his bow and arrows. Because of their hunting abilities they were indispensable to the Tahltan and Cascas people. Even during the late 1800s a good Tahltan bear dog brought $100. Curiously, none survived after being moved to other climates. High powered rifles lessened their value, and sadly enough, the species was inadvertently allowed to die out. The last known died in Telegraph Creek in 1971*

Cass shrugged.

"Well, if you get a chance, hide most of it until you leave. I'll leave you the rifle."

"No way. You're the one that will need the rifle."

Scotty bought moosehide boots, one dried salmon, rice, matches and a handful of tea from Charlie. What he didn't buy was snowshoes, a decision he later regretted. This was no ordinary winter!

Saying goodbye to Cass was difficult. Scotty headed down the river without looking back. The weather turned colder, with the savage, infamous north, or "Stikine" wind pushing against his back. This wind draws cold air out of the Interior, blowing downriver, sometimes with terrible velocity.

Another blizzard struck Scotty two days below Charlie's camp. For 24 hours he lay trapped in his canvas shelter, pushing off drifting snow to keep from being buried alive. With visibility less than 50 yards, travel was out of the question. Without the fur-lined moosehide boots his feet would have frozen.

After the storm ended drifts piled 10 feet deep slowed his progress. Finding wood became nearly impossible. He considered returning to Charlie's but Tahltan was the same distance.

That afternoon, with the icy north wind still howling, Scotty was traveling the wind-swept ice over what he though was a shallow part of the river. Suddenly he broke through an overflow, sinking to above his knees. The boots filled with icy water. To keep from losing the boots he had to sit down on the ice in several inches of water and pull them out one at a time. He emptied his boots then hurried ashore. Only snow-covered willow thickets grew near the river. Heart racing, he fought through deep drifts and willow thickets and reached a stand of pine timber. Beneath a big pine windfall he scooped away the snow, removed dry shavings out of his coat pocket, saved from the night before, broke off dry pine branches and struck a match. A gust of wind blew it out. He tried again, and again, but each time the wind extinguished the blaze. His feet and hands were numb. Desperate, he shoved a bullet slightly into the muzzle of his rifle, worked it loose with his teeth from the cartridge, and emptied black powder into the kindling. The fire blazed hot. He searched for wood, breaking off dead branches. By the time a good blaze was burning, his boots and wet clothing were frozen stiff. He sat down in the dry snow and held the boots over the fire until they softened enough to remove. Wrapping his feet in his blankets, he began the long, impossible process of drying his stockings and boots. Several toes had already turned white. He guessed the temperature was 30 degrees below. With the wind chill, it was probably 50 or 60 below. For the second time in as many days Scotty wondered if he could survive.

The northern night set in at four o'clock. He wrapped the blankets and canvas around his shoulders and hugged the fire. Luckily, the windfall caught fire and provided enough heat to last the night. During the long night Scotty decided to cache most of his gold so he could travel faster.

When it was light enough to travel he made tea and chewed dried salmon for breakfast, then began ploughing through the deep snow, looking for a place to cache part of the gold. The country was featureless. Finally he abandoned the plan to lighten his pack and staggered on. Several frostbitten fingers began to throb like a toothache.

With the last of his strength, Scotty stumbled into Tahltan village, a collection of rough shacks and log cabins. Dogs announced his arrival. At the first cabin Scotty pounded on the door. When it opened he collapsed inside. An old Tahltan man and his wife lived there. They helped him out of his pack and fed him hot broth. They couldn't speak much English, but dried his blankets and told him to curl up on the dirt floor behind the stove on a bearskin. He slept for 12 hours, woke up long enough to eat more soup and drink tea, then slept another day.

From the villagers Scotty bought new woolen and fur clothing and a grizzly bear robe. He decided the fur saved his life during the next month of travel. For a quarter ounce of gold he hired a young Tahltan to sled him to Telegraph Creek. When he asked if he'd continue on to Fort Wrangell, the man refused.

Bundled in the grizzly hide on a sled, they reached Telegraph Creek over a well used trail in a few hours. At Millers trading post Scotty caused quite a stir, especially when they learned where he'd came from. He found several miners who had fled the winter at Dease Lake. They were broke and, because the last boat had departed, were trapped in this isolated location for the winter. He made a deal with two men that he thought he could trust to accompany him down the frozen river to Fort Wrangell. He bought provisions, a sled and three dogs, At $100 each, all that were available, and other necessary camping equipment.

When he paid with gold there was more excitement among those present in the store. He told them that he and his partner had found only a small amount of gold "up the Tuya." His partner was expected to show up soon on a Tahltan's sled.

Miller warned that only fools would attempt going down the river this early in the season and they would either fall through the new, treacherous ice, or be trapped by open water near the mouth. Scotty agreed, but had to reach the nearest doctor, 900 miles away in Victoria.

Traveling 160 miles over new river ice was a frightening experience. The roar of fast water and tumbling rocks beneath the ice was a constant reminder that their survival depended upon their ability to "read" ice conditions. Where the ice was sound and snow-free they made excellent time, with Scotty bundled in furs on the sled. Where the current ran fast and the ice was unsafe, they were forced to take to the shoreline, fighting brush, windfalls and devils club. Progress, especially with the sled, was painfully slow during these portages.

They entered a canyon half a mile in length. Open water was ahead so they had to detour around sheer cliffs several hundred feet high. The detour took three days and sapped all their strength. By the time they reached the river again Scotty was crawling and his partners so tired they could hardly walk.

They expected to find game but the country was devoid of animals. Bears were asleep for the winter. Moose had fled to easier places to find food.

Scotty's companions were not the cheerful men he thought. They argued endlessly about every decision, frightened they would never make it to Wrangell alive. They threatened to leave Scotty and return to Telegraph Creek after the ice grew thicker. Both were unarmed, having traded their rifles for food, but they could easily have killed Scotty with an axe, or taken his rifle and gold, then dumped his body through a hole in the ice. No one would ever know. If they got out alive, they could simply report he died on the river. There would be no inquiry. Fortunately, the men were not murderers, but their threats were discomforting. They demanded to be paid so much a day. Scotty refused, believing if he agreed, they would keep on pestering him for more, or simply take what gold he had. They already knew that Scotty's heavy pack contained more than a "little" gold.

One night one of the men lifted Scotty's pack, looked at his companion, laughed, then told Scotty if he wanted them to help him to Wrangell, he'd have to cut them in on his find. Otherwise they were returning to Telegraph Creek.

Scotty knew a bluff when he heard one, but agreed, providing he didn't have to divulge the location of the mine until after they reached Fort Wrangell. He decided that statement probably saved his life.

Ten miles from the mouth, tidal conditions broke up the ice at high water. The salty slush ice refroze during slack tide, but was unsafe, forcing them ashore. Tangles of devils club, alder and willow made progress painfully slow. They abandoned the sled. Since they had no dog packs, or food for the dogs, they shot them one at a time for food. The starving animals were unfit to eat, but they ate them anyway. To make matters worse, a cold wind blew down the river and rain and sleet fell, soaking their clothing. Scotty had lost track of time, but thought the trip took three weeks.

They reached the ocean at Green Point, four miles across the channel from Fort Wrangell. A southeast storm was blowing and whitecaps raced through the channel between the river and the tiny village.

They set fire to a cedar snag, which burned for several days. Their food was gone. Scotty loaned his gun to one of the men and he shot a harbor seal. They roasted the blubber and seal meat over the coals. The seal's liver was delicious.

After four days the wind stopped. A large Tlingit canoe, paddled by four husky Indians arrived. They were curious about the fire. The Indians were astonished that the men had made it safely down the river from Telegraph Creek so early in the winter. Scotty paid them a pinch of gold when they arrived in town.

There was no doctor in the village. One old Tlingit Indian served the community as midwife. She took one look at Scotty's feet, held her nose and shook her head. "Soak every day in cold water and Epsom Salt," she said.

Scotty was lucky. A ship, the last southbound ship of the season, was detained because an engine part had to be replaced. All berths were taken. The purser saw how bad Scotty's condition was, and allowed him on board and provided him with a cot in the hold. His two companions decided to stay in Wrangell. The unheated hold reeked with the smell of tar, raw furs, empty whiskey barrels and Scotty's feet. Scotty was thankful for warm fur clothing and robes he had bought in Tahltan. He stayed in bed during the entire voyage.

The voyage south was a stormy one, and the ship was forced to take shelter from severe southeast winter gales. Scotty bribed the cook to deliver soap and warm water once each day in which to soak his feet in Epsom's Salts. One foot had turned black and toes on the other were slowly rotting.

At Victoria Scotty couldn't walk and had to be carried to the hospital. Doctors took one look and announced that it was a miracle he was still alive. They cut off one leg above the knee, the toes on the other foot, one thumb and a total of five fingers.

The GERTRUDE, Captain William Moores favorite boat. She's 120 feet in length. Built by Moore in Victoria in 1875 and went right to the Stikine River, where this photo was taken by Mr. Dossetter in 1881. Sold to Calbreath, Grant and Cook, Cassiar merchants in 1882. Eventually owned by Captain John Irving and used primarily on the Fraser and Stikine.

Scotty sent a message to his lady friend. She came to the hospital. Scotty gave her a nugget. She smiled. Then he pulled up the sheet and showed her his stump of leg. She took one look, the nugget and that was the last Scotty saw of her.

Captain Moore and his sons stopped by and slid a bottle of rum under his blankets. Moore listened to Scotty's story silently. Such hardships were nothing new to him. When Scotty finished, Moore pressed for more information about the gold Scotty and Cass had located.

Scotty refused to admit that they'd found more than the usual two-bit pans. The claims had not been staked and recorded. If anyone knew what they'd found, there would be a great rush into the country. Scotty knew enough about Moore's business practices to know that if he learned the truth, he's spread the word that another rich strike had been made just so he would have more business on the Moore Trail.

Then Moore dropped a piece of news that startled Scotty. Business had been brisk for the Moore family in 1874. Between tolls on the road and his boys mines, they'd came out with $50,000 and were building a new 120-foot-long paddle wheeler, the *Gertrude*.

Johnnie smiled. "You should have taken the lay I offered you. I let it to a man from New Westminister. That piece of ground was worth $5,000!"

"I guess so," Scotty said, stunned.

"What about Cass?" Captain Moore wanted to know.

"Hopefully he'll show up."

"From the way you describe his condition, I wouldn't want to bet on it. But we'll hope so." After the Moores left the hospital, Scotty realized that Captain Moore's keen nose for gold had detected a scent in Scotty's story. He'd have to be careful, or the Fishhook Lake area would become another Dease Creek overnight. He resolved that he'd not let Captain Moore know any more than he already had, until those claims were staked and recorded.

Learning to walk with crutches, waiting for a wooden leg to be made, practicing to write with missing fingers, in shock after his near-death experience, and worried about Cass, he found a room and settled down to recuperate. It was a long, miserable winter.

Chapter Five

✦

Return to the Cassiar

S pring came early in balmy Victoria. Dogwood bloomed in mid-March and flowers in front of buildings lining the Inner Harbor added welcome color to boardwalks along the muddy street.

Scotty hired a horse-drawn buggie to attend the gala event of the spring, the launching of the *Gertrude* at Laurel Point, March 22, 1875. Mrs. Moore, their daughters and sons were all present, and a daughter swung a champaign bottle to start the beautiful new ship sliding down the ways with a splash. A great cheer rang out. Champaign flowed and Captain Moore was toasted. Victorians, except perhaps for several ex-creditors standing in a small group, had almost forgotten that only a decade before Moore had declared bankruptcy and lost everything.

Moore noticed Scotty standing on his crutches and came over to shake his hand. "What do you think of her?" he asked.

"She's beautiful. Congratulations. Yours is a real rags to riches story."

"Perhaps a rags to riches to rags story," Moore laughed, "Who knows?" He slipped a bottle of champaign from under his coat and presented it to Scotty. "Maybe this will help you remember where your rich mine is located. Why didn't you record it?"

"How did you know we didn't?"

"Come on Scotty. I checked, that's why."

"Well, like I said, we just picked up a bit of gold here and there."

"If that's the case, I better take some men and follow your trail."

"It's a free country."

"Where did you get that rich mine idea?" Scotty scoffed.

"According to the moccasin telegraph, you came down the river with a very heavy pack."

Scotty laughed. "In my condition, 20 pounds would have been a heavy pack. Hell, I'm lucky to be alive. I do have just enough to buy passage north to look for Cass. What is the sailing date?"

"April 15. And this ship has enough horsepower to steam right up to Telegraph Creek."

"Really!"

By mid-April the oak and maple leaves had budded out. In the Cassiar aspen and birch leaves wouldn't even bud until June or July. The location of the mine was about 4,000 feet, much higher elevation than Dease Lake, elevation 2,600 feet. Scotty was still sick, and in no condition to head into the wilderness, but felt obligated to look for Cass.

He took only a small outfit, undecided what would transpire until he determined Cass' fate, and boarded the *Gertrude* amidst the hustle and bustle of sailing. The ship was packed with people, 50 horses and freight. Much to Scotty's amazement, several tourists were on board, including one dowager dressed in furs and feathers. They settled in for the excursion in fancy, first-class main-deck staterooms.

The *Gertrude* blew a series of long, melodious blasts on her steam whistle as she churned out of the Inner Harbor in a cloud of black coal smoke. She was fast alright, and Captain Moore didn't ease back on the throttle as they steamed up the Inside Passage.

At Wrangell, Scotty couldn't believe his eyes. Since last winter the place had grown, with new, false-fronted saloons and dance halls lining the muddy street. Captain Moore would have liked to bypass Wrangell because United States Customs inspectors had been giving him problems with freight from Canada, but he stopped long enough to clear.

Since little transpires on the Stikine River that Wrangellites don't know about, he inquired if any word had filtered down the river about Cass. Nothing had.

The *Gertrude* steamed over the bar and into the river at high tide against the spring runoff. It was an unusual, clear spring day. Scotty sat on deck and watched the rugged country slip by. Places where he and his companions had recently spent days crawling over cliffs now passed by in a few minutes. How beautiful the country was from the decks of a ship. Salmon leaped, bald eagles perched on cottonwood, bears walked the shores, an occasional moose was seen feeding in shallow ponds and glaciers poured icebergs down lofty mountains, some almost reaching the river. Quite a contrast to how cold, ugly and cruel it had been during the winter.

The tourists used their telescopes and binoculars and took their high tea on the main deck. Each evening the first-class passengers joined Captain Moore in the officers dining room. He entertained them with countless stories about gold strikes, adventures in Peru, hauling barges across northern British Columbia with horses and by hand to the Omineca gold fields and being shot at by Indians while barging up the Skeena River.

People at Telegraph Creek were surprised to see Scotty alive. They assumed all three men had died on the river. They were also intensely curious because he brought an outfit. Did he intend to return to the Tuya? Was it worth their time to stake? There had been much speculation around the huge wood-burning stove in the trading post during the long winter about Scotty's statement that he had found gold on the Tuya, considered to be barren of the precious yellow metal.

Scotty assured them that he had only returned because he was obligated to find Cass. No one in Telegraph Creek knew anything about the missing man. Several natives were at the trading post. Scotty inquired if they knew a white man, called Cass, that had wintered on the Tuya. Or if they knew Charlie? They shook their heads, pretended they didn't understand English, and drew away.

Scotty quickly learned that riding horseback with a wooden leg was difficult and uncomfortable, until one of the Moore boys made a socket instead of a stirrup for the stump of his leg. Even then riding caused him great discomfort. Following the pack train loaded with freight, Scotty stopped at Tahltan, to visit the natives that had fed him the previous fall. They were surprised to see him alive. Scotty brought them presents, a warm Cowichan sweater for the old lady and a pipe and smoking tobacco for the man. Scotty inquiring if they had seen his partner, Cass, that he had left with a trapper named Charlie last fall on the Tuya. No one had. Did they know Charlie and Lenora? They looked at one another, shrugged and pointed north. "That way," they said. Scotty knew they were avoiding his questions, afraid their tribesmen had done something wrong.

Scotty was amazed at how much work the Moore crews had accomplished the previous year. This season they were going to replace the pedestrian bridge across the Tahltan. Horses were forded across downstream of the bridge.

At Dease Lake Landing Scotty talked to a Mountie that had wintered there who assured him that Cass hadn't been seen. People who had wintered at Dease Lake assumed he and Cass had both died when they didn't return the previous fall. There were no plans to search for them.

The Mountie reported it had been an exceptionally early, hard winter with double the amount of snow and record cold. Temperatures at Dease Lake had dropped to 50 below zero and stayed there between Thanksgiving and Christmas. The mines were still closed because of a lack of water. Reports from hunters indicated many wild animals had died.

Three years had passed since the initial gold strikes at Thibert Creek and Dease Creek, but only two seasons after any extensive mining had been accomplished..

Laketon, he was told, boasted the "best" hotel between Victoria and Dease Lake, whatever such dubious comparison meant. Probably because it was the only hotel between those two places! Substantial wood and log buildings were spread out along the lake front, amongst cottonwood, spruce, birch and quaking aspen. Sturdy buildings were mandatory if one intended

Dease Lake Landing, south end, or head of the lake, 1930. Peaked-roofed building was RCMP Post, still standing in 1996. Large building was Hudson's Bay Trading Post. c.1930

to spend the winter, where temperatures often dipped to 50 degrees below zero. There was a Northwest Mounted Police jail, a blacksmith shop and Hudson's Bay trading post containing, besides the essentials, typical "foofaraw" of the period, celluloid collars, music boxes, high button shoes, etc. Bacon was $1 a pound, flour $1.75, beans the same and whiskey was two-bits, or 50 cents a drink. Prices compared to an average wage of $17.00 a month for laborers in the mines! Working hours were 12 hours a day, six days a week. Gold prices were $17 an ounce.

Disappointed, Scotty returned to Telegraph Creek and tried to hire a horse packer to take him up the Tuya in search of Charlie's camp. The packer refused, claiming the river was unsafe for travel, the country too rough, or too swampy for horses. There was no trail up the Tuya, and they needed their horses for the Moore Trail.

His leg was sore where the wooden leg joined above the knee, from riding horseback, and he was sick with the flu. Scotty had no intentions of returning to the mine in his condition, especially after being told there was so much snow in the high country it didn't appear anyone could travel there until late summer. Discouraged, Scotty caught the next boat down the river, then sailed to Victoria. He bought a small log cabin along the Upper Gorge and tried to settle down for a long period of recovery. He tried to banish the gold fever from his mind. Due to his amputations, he couldn't find work. He whiled away the time by reading and playing cards.

Credit: B.C. Provincial Archives, #B-08323

Looking down the Stikine River over historic Telegraph Creek. the town boomed during several gold rushes startling in 1862, but reached its peak during the Klondike rush of 1897-98, when some 5000 stampeders chose the route to Dawson City and Atlin. During the height of the rush, 26 river boats vied with each other to haul passengers and freight from Wrangell 160 miles up the river to head of navigation. In the lower left hand corner is the historic St. Aidan's Church (Anglican). During the construction of the Alaska Highway in 1942, the town briefly boomed again as construction equipment and supplies were carried up the river. Rivers that penetrated the Coast Range of Mountains were the only access to the Interior for centuries until highways were constructed. This photo was probably taken during the late 1900s.

Despite his near-death experience on the Stikine Plateau, the north country was in his blood. Before gold was found in the Klondike, Scotty sold his cabin and returned to Wrangell. He had mastered his wooden leg and still believed he might locate Cass, or what became of him, or perhaps find a partner he could trust and return to the mine and the gold left at "Dead Mule Cache." Doctor bills had sapped his reserves of gold and he was worried about money for his future.

Captain Moore felt sorry for him and gave him a purser's position on the *Gertrude*, paying only half what the purser usually got. Scotty humbly accepted. At least he received food and lodging, and there was always a chance he might learn something about Cass. The vessel alternated between the Stikine and Fraser.

Moore was hounded by debt. By 1880 the Cassiar was about cleaned out. In 1882 Moore was forced to sell the *Gertrude* to J.C. Calbreath, Grant and Cook, Cassiar merchants. It was a sad time because the *Gertrude* held a special place in both Scotty's and Captain Moore's hearts. Of all the 18 vessels he owned, she was his favorite. Scotty was out of a job.

Despite the forced sale of the *Gertrude*, Moore, with his usual unending energy and enthusiasm, bounced back and built the 90-foot *Pacific Slope*. It was a futile effort, however; by the end of 1882, Moore was forced to sell the new vessel. His shipyard, home, three town lots in Victoria, another residence occupied by his son-in-law, Captain William Meyer, even his furniture were sold by creditors. After being in B.C. for a quarter of a century, Moore was flat broke. Most men would have given up, but not this spunky giant of a man.

To make matters even more galling, Captain John Irvine, longtime competitor and fellow ship owner, with whom he had been having fare wars with on the Fraser River, now owned both the *Western Slope* and the *Gertrude*.

Scotty managed to find work as a flunky with Captain Irvine, and was on boats that plied the Stikine River during the Klondike rush starting in 1897.

Captain Moore was down, but not out. Under his son-in-law's name, and with backing of several partners, he laid the keel for yet another, and last vessel, the 130-foot screw steamer *Teaser*. When creditors attempted to take that, he decided to steal her from his creditors. He placed his son Billie on board as captain and ordered him to sail to Petropavlovsk, on the Kamchatka Peninsula. Unfortunately for Moore (and perhaps fortunate for Billie, because it was a dangerous undertaking in more ways than one) Billie put in at Tongass, south of Ketchikan, Alaska, for fuel. The vessel was seized and returned to Victoria, where she was sold for $5,500. This would be the last ship owned, for however short a time, by Captain Moore. True to form, Captain Moore, his son Ben and son-in-law immediately went to Seattle and began construction of the 80-foot stern wheeler *Alaskan*, built under contract for Calbreath, Grant and Cook. Captain Moore and Ben operated the vessel on the Stikine for a time in 1886.

Although Scotty didn't exactly consider Captain Moore a close friend, he was saddened to see Moore's fame and fortune melt away. Scotty thought Moore's problems were his bull-headedness and stubborn nature and refusal to consider people's feelings.

Moore, in his seventies, was finished with steam boating. But he wasn't through with chasing gold strikes. Although the following brief account of Captain Moore's later adventures may be aside from our story, it serves as an additional example of the difficulties of communication and travel of the period.

In 1887, Captain Moore and Skooum Jim, the Tagish Indian who a decade later co-staked discovery claims on Bonanza with George Carmack, claims that started the Klondike Gold Rush, discovered what would later be named White Pass, an alternate to Chilkoot Pass into the Yukon headwaters. Moore was positive tons of gold would eventually be found in the Yukon, and he correctly visualized the preference of this pass over the dangerous Chilkoot, and a town at the present location of Skagway. So sure, he preempted the land for the townsite, but couldn't get anyone interested in financing either the trail or town.

Ben Moore had already gone into the Yukon on a prospecting trip in 1895 with a party of miners, transporting five tons of equipment over the still unnamed pass his father had discovered.

In 1896, age 74, Moore secured a Government contract to deliver Royal mail from Juneau to Fortymile, a mining camp 600 miles down the Yukon. This was the first contract to deliver mail into the Yukon Valley. For this he received $600!

Transported over Chilkoot Pass, with an unknown number of packers, went 104 pounds of mail, provisions for the entire trip, nails and enough lumber to build a flat-bottomed river boat at Lake Lindeman. This writer has backpacked over Chilkoot Pass and wonders how anyone could carry long boards up the Golden Stairs!

Some 10,000 boats, mostly made of whipsawed native spruce and pine, would be built on the shores of Lakes Lindeman and Bennett by 1898.

Moore then proceeded to deliver the mail. Then, in his little flat-bottomed boat, continued down the entire 2,100 miles to Saint Michael, the mouth of the Yukon. He caught a ship to San Francisco, returned to Victoria and prepared to do it all over again! He departed in August for another mail trip to Fortymile. This was pretty late to be going on a trip of that length.

On this second trip, at the present site of Dawson City, Captain Moore made the greatest blunder of his career. He camped overnight on the beach and met George Carmacks. Carmacks explained that he, Tagish Charlie and Skookum Jim, had just staked three discovery claims on Rabbit Creek, a tributary to the nearby Klondike, and the showing looked very good. He invited Captain Moore to hike up and stake. Rabbit Creek would later be known as world-famous Bonanza Creek, which with surrounding creeks, would produce $100 million and lure some 75,000 hopefuls into the country. For unexplainable reasons, Moore declined.

Now, this great pioneer, the man with a nose that could scent new gold, who was only a few hours walk from Carmack's discovery claim, this man who had vowed to never be late for another gold strike did an extraordinary, unexplainable thing. He proceeded on and continued to Fortymile, a clump of 200 cabins, largest settlement in the Yukon Valley and where all mining claims for the region were recorded.

At Fortymile there was a strong rumor that a new discovery had been made. William Ogilvie was present, and sent a letter to the Dominion government to that effect with Moore. So he had to have known!

Was it because he was under contract to carry the mail on down to Fortymile and Circle City? Was it because it was late in the fall and he was worried about catching one of the two last river boats of the season, the *Arctic* and *Bella*, that were somewhere below Circle City? The *Bella* was scheduled to meet the southbound *Bertha* at Saint Michael on October 1. Was it because he had became jaded by too many gold strikes? Or was it because he just thought it was another so, so gold strike?

Whatever the reason, it was costly. He could have taken a day off, hiked up to Rabbit Creek, staked, then filed upon reaching Fortymile, and become a millionaire. In fact, one of Moore's friends staked a claim on Bonanza in his name, but it was jumped because it was known he hadn't been there in person, and turned out to be a rich claim.

It seems odd, but none of the Moore boys were to get rich in the Klondike either. Billie was fishing and trading with Natives on the lower Yukon. Ben had returned to Juneau where he had married a Native. Henry and three companions had sailed for Alaska in the schooner *Sea Bird* in 1886. They anchored in Blinkinsop Bay to await favorable tide down Johnstone Straits. While they slept Indians came aboard, murdered all four men and sank the vessel.

As if in punishment for Moore's neglect to stake at Bonanza, reaching Saint Michael became impossible because of freeze-up. Trapped in the Yukon for a winter wasn't for him, a strong family man. He wanted to go home. At Fort Yukon he turned back. Imagine how disappointed he must have been to know he faced a long, difficult trip out. It was November, but the river ice was still unsafe, so he was forced to wait until it froze solid enough to travel on. He bought dogs and a sled, then on the trip upriver again camped at the mouth of the Klondike River a second time. He spent four days resting his dogs, and STILL didn't go up to Bonanza and stake a claim! In mid-winter cold, with several companions who wished to escape Dawson, they sledded to Lake Bennett, then crossed Chilkoot Pass in mid-January, an almost unthinkable act, especially for a man in his seventies. This writer backpacked Chilkoot Pass in June. Thoughts of doing so in the winter are more than just chilling, it is downright frightening. This Pass experiences terrible storms and there's no wood for fuel.

Scotty kept track of Captain Moore's whereabouts through Captain John Irving and Mrs. Moore in Victoria. During the summer of 1898, at the height of the Klondike Stampede, 56 steamboats ascended the Yukon carrying 7,540 tons of supplies to the near-starved camps. Although Captain W.D. Moore, the second son, was a prominent river boat captain during this season on the Yukon, the senior Captain Moore, so dominant in the earlier river boat business, was not only without a boat, he was absent from the Yukon Valley.

Moore's instincts about staking at Bonanza may have been questionable, but his visions of Yukon riches and the importance of White Pass were, as usual, on target. He and his son Ben preempted land, which was to become the town of Skagway, and built the first wharf. They finally obtained financing to construct a "trail" over the pass, even though it was so bad 3000 horses died on it the first winter it was in use. Not necessarily Moore's fault, but rather that of many inexperience horsemen.

Captain Moore made his last "rush" and joined Billie in Nome for the gold discovery there in 1900. Moore died in Victoria, March 29, 1909 at the age of 87.

Scotty's mining days were over. Scarcely a night passed that he didn't dream of golden nuggets and the rich mine on a mountainside above a fishhook-shaped lake in the Cassiar. He considered a new partnership, then decided no one could locate his mine without him along. If they did find it without him they would surely stake it in their names, since he had no legal claim to it. If he let someone work it on shares, without him to watch cleanup, they would steal him blind. He regretted they hadn't staked and filed the claims before leaving, but the snow storm had made that impossible.

Rumors abounded about the happenings of Captain Moore amongst the river boat men. In fact, during the years just before the Klondike, Moore's absence from his usual haunts caused considerable speculation that a gold strike must be going on somewhere in Alaska or the Yukon. The moccasin telegraph carried bits and pieces about Captain Moore's whereabouts.

Years sped by. Scotty worked on the boats during the summer and wintered in Victoria or New Westminister. When the boats headed north Scotty became restless and usually went along. He was willing to work for a small salary, seeking mostly companionship, a place to stay and food.

In July, 1897, two vessels, carrying a $1.5 million in gold from the Klondike, landed at Seattle and San Francisco and changed world history. The Klondike Gold Rush caused more people to rush to one place than at any time in history. Half a million people converged on the three main routes, Chilkoot and White Passes, and the "all-Canadian route" up the Stikine River, then over the Teslin Trail to the Yukon headwaters. Working on the river boats, Scotty found himself in the thick of the rush and witness to the hoards of crazed, hungry gold seekers who chose the Stikine. Listening to them reminded him of his younger days when he and Cass rushed on stampedes in the Fraser Valley and Cariboo. How many of these cheechacos would never return home, or return maimed for life, he wondered.

Prospectors dog sledding over the ice up the Stikine River.

They started arriving at Wrangell during the winter of 1897-1898 before breakup. Many disregarded the dangers of winter travel over river ice and proceeded up the frozen river with dogs, horses, sleds and backpacks, unwilling to wait for breakup and the river boats. Several disappeared through the ice. But that didn't stop the most eager, who wanted to get the jump on those who would be coming upriver on boats after the ice went out. They didn't realize that, while it was spring in Wrangell, the interior was still locked in winter's icy grip and deep snow for many, many more months.

After breakup, 26 river steamers plied the Stikine that eventful summer, loaded to the gunnels with men, women, dogs, horses, wagons, liquor and other freight destined for the Teslin Trail and the Klondike. Strangely enough, Captain William Moore wasn't among them. Telegraph Creek and Glenora were thronged with people. Most were poorly equipped for life on the trail. There were shootings, robberies

SS Strathcona steaming up the Stikine River.

Pack train ready to depart Telegraph Creek for Dease Lake. Although photo is undated, automobile tires place the time after a road was built between Telegraph Creek and Dease Lake Landing in 1928.

and people who were willing to fight each other to be first to reach the Klondike, unaware, of course, that the good ground had already been staked, and had been since late 1897, by miners who were already at Fortymile, or in the vicinity of Dawson City when the strike was found.

Gold fever was rampant. Five thousand stampeders poured up the Stikine. Three thousand five hundred actually traveled the Teslin Trail that spring. Many turned back, reporting snow ten feet deep and bitter cold, even in June. The trail was littered with discarded belongings, and several dead bodies no one could bury because of the frozen ground. Those who turned back may have been the lucky ones.

Scotty never gave up hope of finding out what happened to Cass and his share of the gold. In May, 1897, during the great rush of stampeders up the Stikine, Scotty was working as a dishwasher and flunkie on the Canadian Pacific Railway steamer *Ogilvie*. To Scotty's delight, the vessel was under the command of Captain Billie Moore, fresh back from the Yukon.

At Telegraph Creek a familiar-looking Indian and his wife came aboard with large bundles of furs. It was unusual for Natives to take furs to Wrangell, where they hoped to find a better price than they'd been offered at Calbreath's trading post. It was customary for the Indians to run up a store bill at Telegraph Creek during the summer and then bring in their furs the following spring to settle up.

Scotty though he recognized them, but was unsure where he'd seen them before. Suddenly he remembered. Two decades had changed their appearance. Finally he approached them and said,"Hello Charlie.,"

Charlie seemed surprised. He didn't recognize the crippled old man either.

"I'm Scotty. I and my partner Cass stopped at your camp on the Tuya. Remember?"

Charlie nodded, looked uneasy, but had nothing else to say.

"My partner, Cass. What happened to him?"

The Nanaook Edserza trapping party somewhere in the Cassiar. Note the Tahltan bear dog coming around the front of the sled. These specialized dogs were invaluable and trained to distract black or grizzly bears while the hunters gathered weapons to kill them. Efforts to move the species out of the Northern B.C. and breed them elsewhere have proven fruitless. Also note the Labrador retrievers used as sled dogs and for carrying packs during summer.

"He left."

"Cass couldn't walk, remember? Scotty showed Charlie his wooden leg and missing fingers. Charlie backed away, his eyes showing fear.

Lenora interrupted. "I speak better English than Charles. I'll tell. After you left there was much snow. Terrible cold. My brother-in-law come with sled. Cass paid gold to take him out."

"When was that? How long after I left?"

"One moon. Maybe."

"Did Cass make it out?"

Charlie and Lenora looked sad.

"Is Cass still alive?"

"My brother, one of his sons and Cass started down the trail.

This many dogs." She held up five fingers. "Camping outfit on sled. Stove. Tent. Big storm came. Stikine wind blew many, many days. Much snow and terrible cold. We wait and wait. No one come back. Maybe month, maybe two months, nobody come. Charlie and I took our dogs and went looking, looking. To village. No sign. No one showed up. We came back. Looking for sign. Very bad trip. Much hard wind on river. Blow sled and dogs backwards on ice. Tent blew down. Two dogs froze to death. I froze fingers." She held her right hand.

"What could have happened?"

Lenore and Charlie both shrugged. "Maybe go through ice. Maybe tent catch fire in storm. No come back. Gone. Gone forever. Brother, his son," Lenore said sadly. "And Cass," she added. "All gone."

"Did Cass pay you?"

"In gold."

"Did you know that Cass had heap much gold in pack?"

They looked at one another. Again it was Lenore who answered. "Not so much. One time, Cass outside house. I look in pack. Little bit of gold. This much." She held out her cupped hands. "I put it back. Charlie not steal. Lenore not steal."

"Well, thank you for being honest and for caring for him," Scotty said.

Cass would have retrieved his cache of gold before they loaded him on the sled. If they went through the ice, the gold went into the river. Perhaps they died somewhere in the blizzard? A small fortune in gold spilling out of rotting pokes somewhere in the vast forest. Another mystery of the north. Scotty was relieved to know, after all those years, what had happened to his partner.

Crippled as he was, finding employment was difficult. After the Klondike Rush ended, Scotty couldn't find work. For several years Scotty was hired to watch the fleet of river boats in winter storage at Wrangell. The job paid little, but he lived in a stateroom on one of the boats. Eventually he quit because the cold, damp winters in Wrangell were too much for him. He drifted south to Ketchikan and became a night watchman at a salmon cannery in the bustling new village. The job provided a place to stay and enough salary to live on.

That's where he met Joe Krause, a tall, dynamic Ketchikan resident and World War I veteran. They became good friends. Joe never tired of listening to Scotty spin stories about his mining days, his relationship with famous Captain William Moore, and working on the magnificent paddle wheel steamers.

Others thought Scotty was another bitter old sourdough that had been maimed by the frigid north country and had gone broke with a pick in his hand. Many old timers fit that description, and several were living out their lives in Southeast Alaska where the weather was comparatively mild.

People listened to Scotty's stories in the saloons, scoffed, humored him, clapped him on the shoulder and bought him another beer. Had he came right out and told someone of his fabulous mine, no one would have believed him. He kept his secret.

Chapter Six

✦

The Promise of Gold

Joe Krause was different from the saloon crowd that Scotty associated with in Ketchikan's bars. Joe was very interested in mining and regretted he'd been born too late to join the Klondike Rush. He checked some of Scotty's stories and decided they were true, that Scotty actually had been involved in mining in all those place he talked about, the Cariboo, Barkerville, Horsefly, the Cassiar.

Scotty had grown a chest-length, bushy, white beard, and kept it neatly trimmed. He was quite a popular figure hobbling about town, especially with children, who he kept supplied with hard candy and allowed them to write on his wooden leg. He was lonesome, with no family, but no one offered to invite him into their homes for a meal, or do more than give him a smile and slap on the back, except Joe.

Scotty suffered a bad fall on icy stairs while alone at the cannery one stormy winter night. The cannery superintendent suggested he retire, before something worse happened. Scotty moved to a shack on nearby Pennock Island where he lived on a tiny Territory of Alaska pension. He was in his late seventies. Rent was only $10 a year. By fastening his hands to a bucksaw handle with leather straps, he cut his own wood. Using the same technique on his oars he rowed his small skiff back and forth to town. After the skiff disappeared during a southeast blow, Joe took Scotty on board his own boat to search the shoreline of Gravina and Pennock Islands, but the skiff had disappeared.

After that Joe delivered coal oil, medicine and groceries to Scotty. If Joe found a good Douglas fir log floating in Tongass Narrows, he'd tow it to the beach in front of Scotty's shack and tie it up for firewood.

Joe visited Scotty frequently, and noticed he was failing fast. He required daily pain medicine. There was nothing wrong with his mind, thought. Scotty's favorite drink was hot buttered rum, and he insisted Joe have a drink with him when he came to visit..

One October day, after Joe delivered supplies, the old man told Joe that he was soon "going under", and because Joe was the only true friend that cared about him, he was going to share a secret with him. But the time wasn't right yet.

Joe was consumed by curiosity. What "secret" could Scotty have that he'd be interested in? That winter was particularly cold and stormy. Two feet of snow covered the ground and Tongass Narrows froze over temporarily, until the tide broke up the ice. Gale force winds whistled through Ketchikan and Tongass Narrows. Several weeks went by without Joe rowing across the channel to see how Scotty was doing.

Finally the wind stopped and the weather moderated. Joe bought some groceries, a gallon of coal oil, a bottle of rum and rowed across. No smoke came from Scotty's stovepipe and there were no tracks in the snow around the woodshed. Joe burst into the cabin, expecting the worst.

Scotty was in bed and the stove was cold. Scotty looked up from his pillow. Relieved to see he was still alive, Joe asked, "How you doing?

"Not worth a damn," Scotty replied. "Think I had the flu. Couldn't even start the fire."

Joe poured a shot of rum. "Here. Drink this. It'll warm you up until I get a fire going. That was some blow, wasn't it?"

"Blew like hell. Thought it would blow my roof off."

Scotty sniffed the rum and sat up, leaning back against the pillows. Joe soon had a roaring fire in the stove.

"How long has it been since you've eaten hot food?"

"Quite a spell."

"Well, we'll fix that." Joe went to work cooking bacon and eggs.

After Scotty had eaten, he looked at Joe, eyes filled with tears, and said, "You know, Joe, you and Cass have been my best friends. Poor Cass. I think about him often."

"It's tough to lose a best friend. I lost a few during the war. Scotty, you don't look so good. I think I'll row you across to town, or bring the doctor."

"It won't do. Everyone has to die. I've lived a long, happy life. My only regret is that I never went home to Scotland to visit my dear old mother before she passed away. I also wished I'd married. Now I have no kin, either here or in the old country. I should have married one of those pretty little squaws, huh?"

Joe nodded. "You sure you don't need a doctor?"

"Positive. I'm feeling better already. Pour me another little sip, will you Joe? About them squaws. Some of 'em made mighty good wives. I knew one in the Cariboo. Her name was July. Should have asked her. She was a hard worker and pretty as a picture. Dammit, why I never asked her to marry me I'll never know. I was a handsome young buck then. She'd have done it too."

Joe agreed a good wife was a valuable asset.

"Scotty, you should go to Sitka and enter the Sanitarium at Goddard Hot Springs. They'd take good care of you, and you could soak in the mineral springs every day."

"I ain't going to no sanitarium, or anywhere else."

"Why not?"

"Cause. Everyone would look at my amputations and laugh at me."

"They would not. Probably most of the people there are worse off than you are."

"Not going. That's that."

The hot food and rum revived Scotty. He perked up and said, "Joe, pull up a chair. You're my faithful friend, the only one that cares enough about me to come to Pennock, visit and help me. It ain't gonna be long before I'm gone. Starting today, I'm going to tell you about my mine."

Scotty had mentioned his mine in British Columbia several times, but Joe shrugged it off, thinking it was not important. If Scotty owned a mine he wouldn't be so poor.

"Reach under the mattress on the other side and feel around for a tobacco tin."

Joe did as he asked, and brought out a flat tobacco can, with all the paint worn off. It was surprisingly heavy.

"Dump it on the bed," Scotty said. Five beautiful golden nuggets, one the size of an acorn, rolled out.

"My God. They're beautiful. Where did they come from, Scotty?"

"My mine. In the bottom drawer there's a brown envelope with your name on it. In case I died. Fetch it please, and open it."

Joe did as he as told. A well-used notebook and hand-drawn map were inside.

"Don't look at it. Sit here by the bed. First I want to finish my story. I've already told you about Cass and I having mined in several places. We were the best. We knew our stuff. And we were lucky in the Cariboo, darn lucky. We got on a paystreak and took out $20,000 in two months. Boy! That was exciting."

"But these nuggets came from our mine in the Cassiar. I've told you how in '74 Cass and I went there, with no less than Captain William Moore and his three sons, But we were too late. The Moore boys struck it rich, but all the good ground was gone by the time we got there. Rather than work for someone else, or quit the country, we took a chance and went off on a prospecting trip into the wilderness. North of Dease Lake. Where not even an Indian had been. Least we didn't see any sign of one. God, Joe, that country is beautiful. Full of game in the summer. Deadly in winter. We were young then, Cass and me. We had ourselves a grand time exploring, panning, hunting, fishing." Scotty paused and sipped his rum.

"What I haven't told you, or anyone else, we found the richest mine anyone ever saw. In a few weeks we took out over 60 pounds of gold!" Scotty's eyes lighted up. "Sixty pounds of gold!" he repeated, laughing hysterically. "With only our fingers, pans and a tiny rocker! Course some of it was picture rock. Quartz laced with gold. That we had to cache after Jessie died. It's still there, Joe." He sat up in bed and gestured excitedly. "Did we ever strike it rich!"

Joe was so surprised he could only stare at the old man, wondering whether to believe him or not. He checked the rum bottle, but it was down only half an inch.

Scotty laughed. "Sixty pounds of beautiful, yellow gold, Joe." Most of it nuggets, like these, we picked up with our fingers. You see how rough it is. Rough gold means it hasn't traveled far. Somewhere above our mine, maybe only a few miles away, maybe under the glacier, there's a fabulous rich lode."

Joe was dumb-struck, and began to tremble. Until this moment he had discounted Scotty's talk about owning a mine as an old man's wistful thinking. He held the heavy nuggets tightly in his hand. A peculiar warm glow flowed out of the gold into Joe's hand, crept up his arm and warmed his whole body, causing it to tingle. Joe had always loved gold. He was suddenly struck with the worst possible case of gold fever. His hands trembled, his breath came in gasps and his heart raced. Could Scotty's story be true? But the startling news was yet to come.

"No one, 'cept Cass, me and now you, has ever laid eyes on these nuggets. They're all that's left. I've been saving them all these years as reminders. As if I need reminders. I've never told anyone about the mine. It's still there, I reckon."

Scotty held out his hands for the nuggets, rubbed them between his palms, then pressed them to his cheeks. "I carried these beauties on my back all the way from the wild, high mountains north of Dease Lake to Telegraph Creek, then down the Stikine River to Wrangell. Many was the time I felt like tossing them down to lighten my load. But gold is something one doesn't just throw away."

"That's for sure." Joe got up and put more wood in the stove. What he'd just heard made his dizzy. He could hardly think.

"Now, Joe, you're a strong young man. You're smart, and you could sure use a million dollars. I've chosen you to inherit my mine. I'm going to tell you about it, and then I'm going to explain the map.

"But first, I want you to understand, it's no simple mater of just walking in there and finding the mine. That country is a bewildering place. No country to get careless in. We got ourelves lost without a compass. It cost Cass his life, and it nearly cost me mine." Scotty pointed towards his stump.

Joe had asked him years before how he lost his leg and fingers. Scotty had always replied, "Frozen, while prospecting in the Cassiar."

So Scotty told Joe the story you've already read, but not all at once. He wasn't strong enough for that. Every few days Joe would row across Tongass Narrows with more food and medicine. Scotty would tell more. There was nothing wrong with Scotty's memory. Joe wrote it all down, as best he could, after he got home.

It was a bitter January day, with mixed rain and snow pounding the roof when Scotty finally finished his story and spread out the map.

"I'm giving you the map only if you promise not to go rushing unprepared into the Cassiar looking for the mine. It isn't gonna be easy for you to locate, seeing as how you've never been there. But if you look long enough, you'll find it. We hid the stove a long ways from the lake and left no trace of our camp on the lake shore. The tools, well, they're probably still there where we left them before the blizzard hit. The spring run off has probably filled in our diggings by now. It's been a long, long time."

Joe studied the map carefully. Actually, it was pretty crude and didn't make much sense.

"Now, Joe, you have a wife, so be careful. Don't take any chances with that country. That plateau is as wild as they come and confusing, cause the rivers run every which way. You promise?"

Joe promised. Scotty explained the map, the landmarks, and how to line them up to find the lake and mine, and directions to find Dead Mule Cache.

"Did you stake and register the mine?"

"No. Cass and I talked about it. Because it was in such a remote and unlikely location, we decided not to. If we'd have filed on it there would have been a mad stampede into that country, and we didn't want that until we had time to explore the placer before we staked our claims. We know what wild stampedes are like. They're crazy. While we were there we were so busy picking up gold we didn't have time to look around before the blizzard hit."

Scotty was failing fast. Joe made a few more visits, then had to make a run with his fast boat to the copper mines on the West Coast of Prince of Wales Island. When he told Scotty he would be gone for a week, Scotty drew him close in a hug, then handed him the brown envelope containing the notebook and map. Scotty kept the tobacco can containing the nuggets, claiming when things got bad, it was a comfort for him to hold the nuggets in his hand. After he'd "gone under" the nuggets were to be Joe's.

Joe split a supply of wood and carried in into the cabin. He asked Scotty's nearest neighbor, another old pensioner, if he'd look in on him while he was gone. The two men were not on friendly terms, but he promised he would. Joe took the envelope home and hid it in his shop. He didn't tell anyone, not even his wife. While he was away he couldn't get Scotty's mine out of his thoughts. He almost hit a sunken rock because he was preoccupied about that gold.

When Joe returned, even before going home, he anchored in front of Scotty's cabin and rowed ashore. There was no smoke coming from the stove pipe. The cabin was empty and Scotty was gone. Joe searched the cabin. Everything of value had been removed, including the nuggets. The neighbor said Scotty had died a couple of days after Joe's last visit. He had sent word to the authorities in town. A United States Marshal and medical examiner had came, searched the cabin, then departed with the body and a cardboard box of Scotty's belongings.

The marshal told Joe that Scotty had left a note on the table. He showed it to Joe. In a peculiar scrawl, written by holding the pencil in the grip of his fist, Scotty admitting he had falsified his citizenship in order to get a pension from the territory of Alaska, and was a Canadian. He'd always felt guilty about that. He wrote that he had no living relatives or kin in the United States, Canada or Scotland and requested that all possessions of value be given to Joe Krause, his remains cremated and the ashes given to Joe to be scattered on Tongass Narrows. The marshal presented Joe with a box of Scotty's possessions and an urn. Joe looked through the box. There were no nuggets, or anything else of value.

Chapter Seven

♦

Joe's Dilemma

Joe felt bad now that Scotty was gone. He wished he had the nuggets to hold. He was sure Scotty's neighbor had stolen them, but had no proof. The nuggets would have been a welcome reminder that Scotty's story was real, although Joe was convinced. Busy with his own business, he tried to put the mine aside, but thought about it constantly, planning and day dreaming about finding the gold and what he could buy with it.

He studied Scotty's crude map until he knew it by heart. One thing that worried him, though, the map was incomplete after Dead Mule Cache. Only the route from Dease Lake to Caribou Pass and the Fishhook Lake Mine had been sketched, and frankly, it was not only crude, but lacked the detail anyone else needed to retrace the route. Joe readily understood why. After leaving Dead Mule Cache, they'd been lost, then, without a compass, too occupied with carrying the heavy packs and finding a route out of the country to worry about keeping the map updated.

In his spare time he began researching the Cassiar. While sketchy information was available about the Dease Lake Mining District, he found nothing about the area north of there, except it was reportedly rugged, high, unexplored, except for several trails through part of it, unknown, at least to white men.

Joe was no fool. He knew how unforgiving and cruel wilderness travel could be. Such a venture required money, a good outfit, and a trustworthy partner, none of which he had.

Joe operated a transportation service to the West Coast of Prince of Wales Island hauling miners and supplies in his fast, gasoline-powered speedboat. Besides becoming a major salmon producing area, Ketchikan was an important mining town. Copper and gold mines were located on Prince of Wales Island. Most were on the West Coast. To reach them one had to either go around Cape Chacon, the shortest southern route, often impossible during the winter because of southeast gales, or take the much longer way up Clarence Straits and down Summer Straits. Joe was kept busy, and began looking for a partner he could trust to accompany him to the Fishhook Lake Mine. He considered several miners he met, but didn't approach them, because, like many miners, they were heavy drinkers. Joe didn't trust anyone who over indulged.

One place Joe frequently carried blasting powder, supplies and men to was the Tokeen Marble Quarry on Marble Island, in Sea Otter Sound. Tokeen had a post office starting in 1909 until the quarry was abandoned in 1938. The company had a contract to cut marble to built the capitol building at Olympia, Washington, so they had a big crew working. While at the quarry, Joe was always invited to the cook house for a meal.

One day he met a dapper, cigar-smoking young German by the name of Hugo Schmolck. Hugo was the steam engineer on the huge coal-fired boiler that provided steam for the winches used to lift blocks of marble and skid them to the landing to be loaded on barges.

While drinking coffee, Hugo mentioned that he would be laid off as soon as the job was finished. He planed to start his own heating business in Ketchikan, and needed to make some fast money. They talked about mining in general. The local mines were all hard rock, and that required a large investment. When their discussion shifted to placer, Hugo's eyes lighted up.

"Placer, that's a poor man's game. I could get excited about that."

On the next trip, Joe approached Hugo again, and asked him if he could keep a secret. He asked Hugo to swear that he wouldn't divulge anything he was going to say, then told him he knew about a rich placer gold mine that might make them both rich. It was located in the wilds of British Columbia. Hugo was interested. Joe promised to tell him more when the time was right.

"Don't mention a word about the mine. I'd be hounded to death," Joe said.

Venturing into the wilds of Northern B.C., even during the 1920s, was not something to be taken lightly. A rich placer discovery had been made on Pine Creek near Atlin Lake by Frederick (Fritz) Miller and Kenneth McLaren in 1898, during the same period as the Klondike Gold Rush. The Pine Creek strike had caused a lot of excitement in extreme Northern British Columbia and at Juneau, Alaska. Except for the government-built Teslin Trail, and the Telegraph Trail, most of the snowy Stikine Plateau remained as wild and unexplored as ever in the 1920s. A few big game hunting parties frequented parts of the area close to the Stikine and Atlin for a few weeks in the fall.

The Moore Trail had been improved to a wagon road between Telegraph Creek and Dease Lake. The Teslin Trail was abandoned as a route to the Yukon after the White Pass and Yukon Railroad was completed.

Although Joe obtained what maps of the area he could find, most were variations based upon Dawson's survey of 1888, on which Atlin Lake did not even appear. Not until 1893 did this lake, 80 miles long, appear on maps of northern British Columbia. Huge areas were marked unexplored, including most of the huge Stikine Plateau, 20,000 square miles. The lack of a good map certainly didn't encourage Joe to attempt the trip.

In August, 1920, Joe read in the newspaper that four U.S. Army aircraft landed at the George Ball ranch near Glenora. Ball was one of the first to see the advantage in using airplanes for prospecting, and big game outfitting in remote areas. This news fired Joe's ambition to look for the mine by air. However, little was known about landing and takeoff at high elevations with the "flying boats" of this period.

In 1924, more news from the Cassiar caught Joe's attention. Another gold strike occurred on Deloire Creek a tributary of Thibert Creek, running into Dease Lake from the north, only miles from the former site of the big strike of 1872 and Porter's Landing. Even George Ball, who had worked diligently to establish a ranch near Glenora, temporarily abandoned his place and was reportedly mining at Deloire Creek.

Unknown to most miners in the area during the early 1920s, a soon-to-be infamous outlaw was also living along Thibert Creek. He was known there by the name of Arthur Nelson, but changed his name later to Albert Johnson, and became widely known as the "Mad Trapper of Rat River," responsible for one of the largest manhunts in the north after he killed several Mounted Police.

Joe heard about the new strike, which reinforced his belief that the whole area held gold, although Thibert Creek was a long ways, and in another drainage from Scotty's mine.

Joe had served in the Army Air Service during World War I, where he met Lieutenant Roy F. Jones, an aviator. Both men were convinced that air transport was the coming thing, especially in remote areas like Alaska and Canada, where little improvement had been made in transportation during the past two centuries. All commerce still moved either by foot, with horses, dog teams or boat travel.

Joe kept a close watch on news reported in the papers about happenings in the Cassiar. Joe and Jones kept in contact after the war. Joe helped Jones find a job with Standard Oil on a delivery barge that supplied mines, canneries and remote locations around the Ketchikan area.

Without actually telling Jones about the mine, he questioned him on his thoughts about flying into high altitude, remote areas with seaplanes currently in use.

Jones though it could be done, provided the right aircraft was available, then added, it he could obtain financing and find an a plane, he would fly it to Ketchikan and start an air service. After the oil barge job ended, Jones returned south to proceed with his plans. Joe doubted that Jones would be successful.

In June, 1922, Joe received a letter from Jones saying that he had purchased a war-surplus, four-place Curtis MF Seagull with a 180 horsepower Hispano-Suiza engine. It needed some work. At the present time it was inside William Boeing's Lake Union hanger. They planned to install a second-hand engine. He had hired a mechanic, Gerald Smith. They intended to arrive at Ketchikan for the big July Fourth celebration. Would Joe spread the word?

Would he. Within two days everyone knew Ketchikan was to have an airplane.

The only mail service to Ketchikan was the weekly steamer. A second letter from Jones arrived stating he'd under estimated how much time repairs would require.

July Fourth came. Joe was kept busy explaining why Jones wasn't there.

A third letter notified Joe that everything was ready. He'd named the plane the *Northbird*. They were taking off at first light July 7, would stop in Bellingham then Alert Bay. Jones prudently didn't mention when they might arrive in Ketchikan.

Day after day dragged by. Joe wondered if Jones had crashed or been forced down in the wilds along the Inside Passage of British Columbia.

Unknown to Joe, Jones was cooling his heels in Bellingham waiting for smoke from huge forest fires to clear.

Then, on July 17, a Sunday, a telegram arrived from Jones. He was in Prince Rupert and expected to arrive over Ketchikan about mid-afternoon. Would Joe inform townspeople?

Joe looked at his watch. It was already one o'clock. He was in luck. The weekly steamer was due to arrive that afternoon. A large crowd always gathered on the Alaska Steamship Company docks to watch who disembarked, or who was leaving.

It happened that the Pioneers of Alaska were holding their annual convention at the Pioneers Hall. Many important visitors were present from all over Alaska.

Joe spread the word up and down the dock. July 17 happened to be one of those lazy, dry, balmy afternoons, unusual for Ketchikan. Fragrant spruce smoke from the sawdust burner at the nearby Ketchikan Spruce Mills spiraled straight into the air. Deer Mountain loomed behind town, the snow-covered summit shining in the afternoon sun.

Couples strolled arm and arm up and down the docks. Creek Street whores, dressed in the latest Seattle, San Francisco and Vancouver fashions, displayed their wares by parading up and down the dock, pastel parasols twirling. A bright red fire engine drove up and parked on the dock in front of the Alaska Steamship office.

The steamer arrived. Longshoremen caught the heaving lines and pulled in the heavy hawsers and secured them to large bits along the edge of the dock. The gang plank was lowered and a stream of excited passengers disembarked, waving gaily to friends.

Two policemen stood on either side of the gang plank, monitoring who came ashore. During those pre-airline, pre-Alaska State Ferry days, crime was almost non-existent in Ketchikan. Free passenger tickets, known as "pink slips"were sometimes issued to undesirables, with the message to get on the south-bound boat and not come back. Except for undesirables arriving by sea, Ketchikan was a tightly-knit, closed society, and a safe, enjoyable place to live.

Cargo hatches were removed and the cargo booms swung over the holds, lifting sling loads of freight, then lowering them onto the dock, where longshoremen trucked them inside the warehouse.

Joe was kept busy answering questions. Yes, he had known Jones during the war. Yes, Jones would be taking paying passengers for rides. No, he didn't know how much it would cost. Having an aircraft based in town was exciting.

Suddenly the shrill sound of a steam whistle sounded at New England, the farthest south cannery in town. Everyone rushed to the edge of the dock and peered down Tongass Narrows.

"You're looking too high," Joe shouted. "There it is. Over the south end of Pennock Island." More steam whistles joined in. The Spruce Mills, the Alaska Steamship vessel, Ketchikan Steam Laundry on Water Street, then Independent and Sunny Point Canneries all had their steam whistles tied down. Adding to the din was the fire engine's siren.

The *Northbird* cruised down the channel at an elevation of 500 feet. Jones and Smith looked down. Clouds of smoke and steam erupted from several places. The fire engine's red lights were flashing. A huge crowd had gathered.

"A fitting ending to a screwed-up flight," Jones yelled over his shoulder to his mechanic. "The town's on fire." Fires were common in Ketchikan.

He banked into a lazy 180 degree turn and sped back south down the channel, looking for the fire. Then he realized the celebration was for him. He'd worked long and hard for this day. With such a reception, he knew he had been correct. Ketchikan would support his air service. Jones splashed down and taxied to a beach north of Paul Hansen's Store. Joe tossed him a line. Jones climbed out onto the float and gave a bow. A loud cheer came from the crowd.

"What took you so long?" Joe asked, shaking Jones's hand.

"Well, we got caught in the forest fire smoke at Bellingham. Waited two days, and when it didn't clear up we flew to Victoria, then up Vancouver Island to escape the smoke. At Alert Bay, while heading for a beach by the fuel dock, I hit a rock and punched a hole through the nose. Spent a week patching the hole. Flew from there this morning, stopped at Prince Rupert for fuel, and here we are."

Jones and Smith were instant heros. Jones was whisked off towards the Alaska Steamship dock on the shoulders of local butcher Lawrence Erickson, "Doc' Walker, Frank Mulally and Joe Krause. As they passed by Paul Hansen's, Jones handed Hansen a paper sack. "Here, Paul. This is for you."

"What is it?"

"A quart of fresh milk from Prince Rupert."

Paul Hansen took the milk inside and set the bottle in a pan of ice. He placed it in the front window with a sign: First Quart of Fresh Milk in Ketchikan, Compliments Roy Jones, owner of Ketchikan's First Airlines. [6]

Jones and Smith were taken to the Pioneer's Hall and asked to relate their historic flight. The place was packed. Joe returned to the plane with Jones and studied its every feature. At home that evening, he retrieved Scotty's map from its hiding place and peered at it for a long time. Could the *Northbird* be the answer to his golden dreams? He thought so.

Without divulging his plans, Joe asked Jones if he thought a flight into the Cassiar high country was possible.

"Why do you want to go?" Jones asked.

"I can't tell you yet, but it could make us both rich."

Jones though for a moment. "Gold. That's high mountainous country. Better alive than rich," he said, admitting his plane was underpowered for such a venture.

"Wait until I make enough money to buy a better engine, then we'll see."

Joe was disappointed because Jones seemed cool to the idea. Perhaps he should tell him about the map and mine. But Joe had taken a solemn vow not to tell anyone, not even his wife, about the rich mine. He knew what could happen if word got around. Men were willing to kill for such information.

Jones was immediately overwhelmed with work. Besides scenic flights for curious customers, he was kept busy flying mail and men to the far-flung mining, logging and salmon cannery camps.

Jones was cutting heavily into Joe's business. With the *Northbird*, he could haul four men, mail and supplies to the West Coast of Prince of Wales Island and be back in three hours. Even with the fastest motorboat in the country, the same trip took Joe

<hr>

[6] *Personal interview with Paul Hanson, 1962*

three days, if he went without sleep. If the weather was bad, the trip might take a week!

Joe cornered Jones one night and pointed to a place on a Canadian map of British Columbia, such as the map was, and saying if they could fly an outfit in there, he knew something that might make them rich.

Jones glanced at the map, then said, "I flew to Wrangell the other day, and made a swing up the Stikine River. Not far, but far enough to see some pretty stupendous, snow-covered mountains in the distance."

"So," Joe asked, "You're not interested?"

"Oh, I'm interested. But, if its all the same to you, I'll just loaf around here at low altitudes until I have more power." Then he confided to Joe that the *Northbird*, constructed of plywood, was soaking up seawater and was heavier than ever, which didn't speak well for high altitude flights.

Joe was disappointed. He had secretly began accumulating an outfit. A sturdy war-surplus tent, cooking equipment, tools, clothing, canned and dried food. He had even made a knock-down sluice box out of spruce lumber. To explain to the curious store clerks and hangers on at the marine supply stores, he said he planned to go on a bear hunting trip up the Unuk River.

Then Jones' plane lost the plug out of the crankcase and had to ditch in Dixon Entrance. On board as a volunteer mechanic was George H. Beck, who happened to be mayor when I moved to Ketchikan. John Munson, a halibut fisherman, owner of the halibut schooner *Atlas*, towed the *Northbird* back to town.

By now, even Joe had cooled about flying into the Cassiar. But Jones and the *Northbird* were soon flying again.

During two summers, Jones kept busy. Then one day Jones took off for Heckman Lake with Fred Patching, manager of the salmon cannery at the lake, and George King, who was along for the ride. They dumped Patching off at the cannery and taxied down the lake. The plane was airborne near the end of the lake when it suddenly stalled and crashed into the water. Jones and

King survived and were rescued by Patching in a skiff, but the plane, except for the engine, was a total lost.

Joe heard the news with dismay. Jones stayed at the Krause home until the Sunday steamer. It was 1923. Joe watched Jones board and thought, there goes my plan. Jones assured him that he would arrange financing and soon have another, better aircraft. Both knew this was a long shot.

In 1923, General William "Billy" Mitchell, Assistant Chief of the Air Service, announced to the world that in 1924 five aircraft would fly around the world. Joe followed this historic flight avidly, especially the part where they flew around Alaska's Aleutian Island Chain. If airplanes can do that, they can surely fly to the mine, Joe reasoned.

Then, in 1925, startling news drifted out of the Cassiar. A Vickers Viking flying boat, an amphibian, equipped with a 400 horsepower Napier Lion engine, flew from Quebec and landed at Dease Lake. News of another gold strike in the Cassiar had been circulating around Southeast Alaska for several months, and this airplane confirmed that something big was in the wind. The plane was under charter to the newly-formed Dease Lake Mining Company. Joe's heart almost stopped while he contemplated if the strike was the Fishhook Lake Mine.

Joe satisfied his yearning to look for the mine by constantly researching the fledgling, but rapidly advancing airplane business. The water-cooled engines of the period were temperamental, prone to freezing, rupturing, then scalding the exposed pilot. Engine valves stems were prone to overheating and lasting only a few days. Mechanics spent half the time working on the planes.

By 1927, both engines and floats had improved. Charles Lindberg's historic trans-Atlantic flight caused a flurry of interest in air travel. Joe kept a clipping file about the *"Spirit of Saint Lewis."*

Nineteen-twenty-eight proved that progress was being made even in the Cassiar. The Moore Trail between Telegraph Creek and Dease Lake was improved into a truck road.

A nine-place Keystone arrived in Southeast Alaska with pilot Clayton Scott and Gordon Graham as mechanic. Although they were frequently in Ketchikan, Joe didn't have the money or time to spend in the wilds of British Columbia at the time.

Then, in April, 1929, an exciting airplane, a Lockheed Vega, named the *Juneau*, a seven-place, high-wing beauty, powered by a 420 horsepower radial, air-cooled engine, flew non-stop from Seattle to Juneau. NON-STOP, newspaper headline read.

Excitement ran high in Southeast Alaska. Joe didn't get to see the plane, but pictures of it were in the paper. The Vega's owners, Alaska Washington Airways, encouraged by the *Juneau's* success, sent a second Vega, the *Ketchikan*, north.

Joe fell in love with the Vega at first sight. He talked to Floyd Keadle, the pilot, who assured him the Vega had the power to fly into the Coast Range. If the lake was big enough, they could land on it.

This was what Joe had been waiting for. He tried to locate Hugo, but he'd disappeared. Joe didn't know what had happened to him. Business was bad. With the Vega operating, few cared to ride with Joe on his "slow" boat.

The Lockheed Vega had a mixed reputation. Pilots and crews swore by it. Some were not fond of this plywood plane. It had several idiosyncrasies that bothered many passengers. While idling before takeoff, gas would dribble from the carburetor into the water between the floats, starting a frisky little fire. Sometimes the carburetor leaked gas back along the fuselage during flight, causing a spectacular Roman Candle effect that extinguished itself as soon as the fuel burned.

If flying at high altitude, where freezing temperatures were encountered, the plywood froze, producing a series of loud pops, like rifle shots, while descending or flying in turbulent air. While the crews paid not the slightest attention to these quirks, many first-time passengers swore they'd never set foot in a Vega again.

In the spring of 1930 four Vegas came north to Southeast Alaska. The *Sitka*, piloted by Gene Meyring, was stationed in

Ketchikan. Joe got acquainted with Gene and was impressed. He decided this was the man that would fly them into the Cassiar.
He had still not heard from Hugo, so decided to look for another partner. He chose a young, out-of-work hard rock miner. Like many miners, he hung out in the bars. Joe decided he would stay sober once out of town. He didn't tell him much, just that he was onto something good and needed a companion.

As soon as the miner learned that flying into the Canadian wilderness was involved, he politely declined. Joe quietly searched for a replacement, but found no one with half the money for the charter. Another year slipped by.

By the summer of 1932 Joe was desperate. Alaska Washington Airways had gone bankrupt. Times were tough, with the Great Depression closing down many businesses.

Then, during Joe's darkest hours, a ray of hope appeared. After an absence of one decade, Roy Jones flew into Ketchikan as a pilot for Pioneer Airways. This new airline owned two SM-8A Stinson "Juniors", the *Northbird* and *Sea Pigeon*.

Jones had forgot about Joe's gold. "The riches are right under our noses," Jones exclaimed. "This airline is going to make both history and money. Buy as much stock as you can afford, and tell your friends to do likewise."

After Jones learned that Joe was still planning to fly into the Cassiar, he pointed at the Stinson. "That's the aircraft that will take you there, or anywhere you wish to go."

Before Joe could find a partner one of the Stinsons crashed. Joe decided to give the other Stinson time to prove itself. Meanwhile, prospective passengers stayed away in droves.

Pioneer Airways quietly sold out to Jim Hickey, a Ketchikan businessman who owned the Yellow Cab franchise. Jones was fired and took a job with the Bureau of Customs. Joe was absolutely mortified. It looked as if his plans were stopped cold.

Hickey didn't know an elevator from a rudder. He regarded his Stinson as a new toy. He renamed his newly acquired "airlines" Ketchikan Airways. During one of Ketchikan's frequent storms, the hanger roof collapsed on the Stinson. Repair work took weeks. Pilot Murrell Sasseen began flying the rebuilt Stinson. A few days later, the plane flipped upside down in Tongass Narrows. Sasseen wasn't badly injured. Hickey, who had envisioned himself a wealthy airline owner, and Ketchikan, whose love affair with airplanes had definitely cooled, were both once again without an airplane.

Running an "airline" in Alaska at the time involved little more than owning an aircraft, and a hat to keep books in. The planes were crude. Floats, for example, still didn't have rudders, an embarrassing feature when the pilot, while landing or taking off, suddenly spotted either a log or fish boat directly ahead.

Pilots were not required to file a flight plan, or even tell anyone where they were headed. Since there was usually only one aircraft in the area at a time, if a plane went missing, there was no other aircraft to search for it.

It wasn't unusual, when looking for an aircraft believed to have gone down, to send fish boats and Coast Guard cutters to comb the beaches and shorelines searching for survivors. Assuming, of course, that someone might have walked down to the beach, or swam ashore. The Morrison-Knutson plane wreck in Boca de Quadra was discovered exactly this way after the pilot was discovered dead on the beach wrapped in his parachute.

Hugo was back in town, still hoping to start a business. Joe convinced Hugo that the only way to reach the mine was to fly. Hugo was scared. Flying was a form of suicide, he exclaimed, although he recognized the value of Joe's plan.

By then Joe was desperate to find someone who would fly them into the Cassiar. Then another pilot, described by Joe only as "Crazy Charlie" showed up in Southeast Alaska and began taking people on rides. We don't know if he was a Canadian, or whether he operated out of Ketchikan, Wrangell or somewhere else.

Finally Joe hired him to make a short, scenic flight up George Inlet and back over Deer Mountain, just to check him out. The man seemed to be a good enough pilot and level-headed, at least while in the air.

While in town, he was quite a rounder. Charlie was a handsome devil. He frequented the clubs, drank excessively and was an excellent dancer. The ladies thought he was God's gift to women.

Joe told Hugo it was time to go to the Cassiar. They had waited long enough. Both needed money. It was now or never, meaning Joe would look for another partner. Hugo, desperate to make some fast money, reluctantly agreed. Joe overcame his hesitation about Charlie, and arranged a flight up the Stikine.

Charlie wanted to know why he wished to go. Joe insisted it was only a prospecting trip. They took a month's food supplies, mining tools, the knock-down sluice box, army surplus canvas tent, rifle, shotgun, and ammunition.

Hugo was nervous. Only thoughts of getting rich convinced him to fly. He peered at the crude aircraft with dismay. They loaded their outfit on the plane under cover of darkness, donned their helmets and took off at first light.

Joe enjoyed the flight to Wrangell, but Hugo's face was drawn and he never once looked down at the beautiful scenery along Clarence Strait.

In Wrangell, Charlie insisted they walk uptown and have breakfast. On the way, he stopped at a saloon and ordered a round of drinks for the three of them. Before Joe could protest, Charlie ordered another round. Finally Joe convinced Charlie to head for the restaurant. While eating, Charlie ordered a beer, then began talking loudly about their trip, the price of gold and flying into remote country.

Joe called him into the men's room and told him to shut up, or they would return to Ketchikan, that big ears had been listening at other tables. They refueled the aircraft, then loaded two five gallon cans of extra gas. A crowd of curious onlookers watched.

Flying over the tidal flats of the Stikine was quite a sight. The river had three channels, with large, forested islands between. The channels were a maze of sandbars and shallows at low tide.

Photo by Peter Corley-Smith. Credit: B.C. Provincial Archives, #F-02456

The Vickers Viking flying machine at Dease Lake, June, 1925, under charter to the Dease Lake Mining Co. Pilots were J. Scott Williams and C.S. Caldwell. Enroute into the Cassiar, Robert Surratt, a well-known cinematographer, filmed for the first time from the air in the north country. Plane similar to Roy F. Jones Curtis MF Seagull, first plane brought to Ketchikan for commercial use.

Following the silvery strand of braided river, they looked down and saw grizzly bear, moose feeding in lily pads in the backwater sloughs and flocks of waterfowl. Glaciers cascaded down almost to the river's edge. The mountains were breathtakingly beautiful, and so wild the sight took Joe's breath away. Charlie wagged the wings over Telegraph Creek and several people waved. They reached the mouth of the Tuya River. Hugo, in the back seat, kept patting Joe's shoulder, motioning for them to turn back. Thoughts of where they were headed was daunting, even for Joe. Steep canyons, swamps, thick brush and an endless expanse of snow-covered peaks surrounded them on all sides. He kept peering down and thinking, Scotty and Cass walked out of here in the winter. Incredible!

Joe immediately realized that Scotty's hand-drawn map was next to useless. Scotty's observations from the ground meant little from the air. There were hundreds of lakes, and Scotty wouldn't have seen most of them while walking out. Worse of all, this area, which Scotty and Cass had walked on their way out, wasn't drawn on the map. Someone who is lost doesn't bother drawing maps. Even if he had, it was doubtful the map would be of value from the air.

They cruised up the Tuya River, passing by many lakes, then a large lake, which apparently was Tuya Lake. Strangely, Scotty had not mentioned this large lake at all, nor did it show on either Scotty's or the government map. The engine began to labor as the pilot started to climb over the steep stair steps of the plateau. The view ahead was even more awesome. An endless number of snow covered mountains rose from the Plateau like mushrooms. A band of wild sheep dashed along a steep mountain slope. A herd of caribou were bedded on top of a level mountaintop. Ahead were several high, snow-covered peaks, laced with glittering glaciers.

The country didn't fit Scotty's description. Joe realized that from the air everything appeared completely different than from the ground. Suddenly it occurred to Joe that he didn't know how far Fishhook Lake was from Telegraph Creek, or even exactly what shape it really was. At eighty miles an hour, they were covering in one hour a distance that had probably taken Scotty and Cass weeks of backpacking. Joe wondered if they hadn't already overflown Fishhook Lake, left it behind, and were entering an even more remote area. He signaled Charlie to turn around. Thinking they were heading back to Wrangell, Hugo smiled for the first time since they'd left home.

Francis E. Caldwell

Joe studied the land below. The country was beautiful, with meadows of grass amidst clumps of birch, aspen and pine. Closer observations, however, disclosed many difficult ravines, bogs and lakes, places described by Scotty that had caused long, miserable detours.

A maze of confusing canyons angled off to the northwest. There were lakes shaped like beaver pelts, lakes shaped like boats, and, surprisingly, several shaped like fishhooks! Joe looked for a fishhook-shaped lake with a high ridge to the south, and a high peak, with a glacier down its west side to the east. From the air, at a high rate of speed, Joe became totally confused.

Joe passed a note instructing Charlie to head east again. Charlie shook his head and shouted over his shoulder, "Find your lake quickly, or I won't have enough gas to make it back to Wrangell."

Ahead Joe saw a lake ahead shaped like a fishhook, with what appeared to be ridge south of it, and high mountains with glaciers to the east. He would have preferred to circle around, looking over the country, but Charlie kept pointing down with his gloved thumb and signaling they had to land.

With a sigh of relief they landed safely, taxied up to the western shore, picked a spot where there was a gravel beach and shut off the engine.

"God!" Charlie said. "What beautiful, desolate country. Are you sure this is the place?"

"Well, Joe said, "It looks right. Except that ridge to the south isn't as high as I expected."

"Well, what you see is what you get. I don't have enough fuel to do anything but head out. You have two choices. Stay here or go back to Wrangell."

While the pilot poured extra gas into his tank, Joe began unloading the outfit. Hugo stood on the shore peering at the beautiful, but desolate mountain scenery, not offering to help.

"Come on partner, give me a hand here," Joe growled, passing freight out of the plane.

119

"I'll help, but I'm not staying!"

"You're not what!"

"I'm going back with Charlie."

Joe's temper flared. "Like hell you are. You can't leave me here alone. You made a deal, now you're going to stick with it."

Joe jumped off the plane and confronted Hugo. Joe was a foot taller, and he was mad enough to fight.

"You can stick your gold up your ass. I don't want any part of this," Hugo spat.

Joe raised his fist to strike Hugo. Charlie stepped between them, a grin on his handsome face. "I knew it was gold you're after. The map was a give away. There's gotta be plenty here, or you'd never have came. Tell you what. I have a business proposition. Cut me in for a third, and I'll do your flying for you, bring in supplies, fly out the gold. Fair enough?"

"Suppose we refuse?" Joe said quietly, expecting this was coming.

Charlie peered around, a smile on his face. "It's a huge country. I hope I can find this place again."

"You bastard," Joe growled. "You're threatening to abandon us?"

"No. I'd never do that. Just offering you a good business deal. Think how hard it would be to operate in a place like this without me and my plane!"

"We'll think about it. Decide when you return at the end of a month."

"Fair enough. You know damn well I'd earn every penny. Operating here without air support would be impossible."

"You have a point there," Joe agreed, looking around and realizing how far from anywhere they were.

Hugo tried to push pass Joe and get aboard, but Charlie pushed the plane off the beach. "Stay here, Hugo, and make us some money," Charlie said, laughing and giving Hugo a shove. "See you in a month."

He spun the prop. The engine caught, back fired, then roared.

Joe had to physically restrain Hugo from jumping into the lake and swimming for the plane. Charlie laughed, lowered his goggles, gunned the engine and took off in a cloud of spray, his bright red silk scarf flying behind in the wind.

They watched the plane circle, dip its wings and disappear west. They listened until they could no longer hear the sound of the engine. Then it was dead quiet. The call of a common loon disrupted the silence. Hugo was the first to speak. "Damn your hide to hell, Joe," he said. "I'll never, ever forgive you, or Charlie, for this."

"After you have a pocketfull of nuggets you'll change your mind." Joe grabbed the axe and went to cut tent poles. Hugo walked down the lake shore and sat on a windfall, staring angrily at the lake.

The crazy, yodel-like laugh of the loon echoed across the lake again. Hugo yelled, "You're as crazy as that loon sounds, Joe." Not until the tent was up, a fire going and supper cooking, did Hugo return to camp.

The following morning, they hurried up the mountain looking for the mine. Late in the afternoon they returned discouraged and tired. There was no trace of the mine, the tools, or the gravel-filled channel Scotty had described.

Joe searched the thickets of birch all around the lake looking for Scotty's stove, or any sign of their old camp. He found no trace any human had ever been there before!

Suddenly the awesome truth of their situation struck like a hammer. In their haste to satisfy the pilot's demands, they had landed on the wrong lake!

Chapter Eight

◆

Stranded

Hugo was beside himself with anger and self pity. He cursed Joe, then himself, as stupid fools. Not only was there no sign of a mine, panning nearby streams resulted in not one flake of gold.

"Well, the right lake can't be far away," Joe said. "We haven't anything else to do. Let's go find it."

"Not me. You go. Those grizzlies will eat your ass for breakfast and use your rifle for a toothpick. I'm staying right here," Hugo growled. "I've gone on one goose chase with you. I don't intend going on another."

They quit speaking. Joe filled a pack with sleeping bag, tarp, gold pan, shovel, food supplies and the rifle, and began systematically exploring the surrounding country. When his food supplies ran out, he'd return to camp. Hugo laughed at him, asking if he had struck it rich yet. Joe ignored the question.

On one stream, ten miles from camp, Joe struck color. Two or three flakes of gold to the pan. Excited, he followed the stream to its headwaters, but everywhere he tested the gravel, it yielded the same. He put one-eighth ounce of gold into a vial and didn't even mention it to Hugo.

Joe shot a caribou half a mile above camp. They ate and ate the delicious meat, then salted, jerked and smoked the rest in a birch bark smokehouse to keep away the pesky blow flies. They hung the meat high in a tree away from bears and flies.

With the right partner, even without finding the mine, Joe could have enjoyed the trip. The country was beautiful and teeming with game. Hugo's attitude turned the adventure into a nightmare. Joe wondered what he had ever seen in Hugo that caused him to choose him as a partner.

Hugo sat in camp, puffing a cigar, swatting flies and mosquitoes with a spruce bough, the shotgun over his knees. A grizzly sow with two cubs was hanging around camp, feeding on the mountainside in plain view. Hugo was terrified of grizzlies. He drank endless cups of coffee, cut wood and kept a big fire going, thinking it would discourage bears. Joe warned him if he didn't watch out, he would use up their wood supply.

Joe never gave up looking for the proper lake. He roamed a wide section of country, climbing every mountain for a view from the top. Joe was so disgusted with his partner he decided if he found the mine, he wouldn't tell Hugo. Instead he'd return later. The landmarks Scotty had provided just wouldn't quite match up, leading Joe to wonder if Scotty had deliberately omitted important features from his map, in case someone searched his belongings. There was also the question of Scotty's description of Fishhook Lake. Did it really look like a fishhook, or just resemble one? The lake they landed on had a little curved end from the air or from above on the mountain. From the ground, it wasn't very noticeable. There was a lot more snow in the mountains than what Scotty had described. Had Scotty arrived during a period of light winter snow? Could the glacier, so important as a landmark, be covered with snow and unrecognizable, because of a heavier than normal snowfall the past winter? Could the mine still be covered by snow?

Joe decided to find out. He set out for the high mountains to the east. For three days he backpacked. The mountains became steeper and the snow deeper. Finally he gave up.

On the way down he shot a fat sheep and camped for two days enjoying the delicious meat. The kill soon attracted a grizzly. The bear came in silently, sniffing and showing no intentions

123

of leaving when Joe shot above its head. Joe took what meat he could pack and fled.

Back at camp, Hugo stated flatly that he didn't believe old Scotty's story. He thought Joe had been duped by a senile old drunk. But, of course, Hugo had never met Scotty.

Rather than argue and fight, Joe ignored Hugo's torments. Joe loved to hunt and explore the beautiful country. Hugo had no interest in anything except getting back to town. Hugo kept count of the days by notching a nearby birch tree. It was a long, miserable month.

Finally the time to be picked drew near. They began speaking civilly to each other again and packed their belongings with a festive air. There wasn't much food left.

On the thirtieth day they were up early, had breakfast and packed their gear. Clouds obscured the sky, and no plane came. They were not surprised. Joe explained that Charlie may have flown into the area, ran into clouds and had to turn back. There was no way of telling what the weather would be in the Cassiar Mountains from distant Wrangell. They waited impatiently for two days for the weather to clear. A big pile of green brush, with dry wood underneath, was kept ready to set a signal fire as soon as they heard a plane.

Across the lake a wolf howled. The rattle of quaking aspen leaves disturbed the silence. The weather turned clear. Still no plane. Joe tried to comfort Hugo by explaining that the weather in Wrangell might be socked in, and Charlie couldn't start his flight. "How could I have been so stupid as to fly," Hugo retorted. "Never again." They listened so intently for the sound of an engine their ears rang.

This went on for a week. A heavy frost fell one night, a disturbing sign. They didn't know what to expect in the way of fall weather at this high altitude.

Joe, familiar with aircraft, decided engine trouble had delaying the flight. Hugo retorted, "That crazy, drunken son-of-a-bitch crashed going back to Wrangell." Joe had considered that himself, but hadn't mentioned it.

To argument their food supply, Joe kept hunting, staying close enough to camp to hear an airplane. He killed another caribou and jerked more meat. Their shotgun shells were nearly gone. On short forays away from camp Hugo had killed many grouse and ptarmigan.

The second week went by with no sign of a plane. Joe told Hugo they should consider walking out. Hugo threw a tantrum, deriding Joe, blaming him for being in such a situation, claiming they would get lost and die of starvation. Hugo didn't like to walk. If they were going to die, they might as well do it here in camp. Joe realized Hugo was frightened half out of his wits with thoughts of walking over ground they'd flown over coming in.

Hugo had brought a supply of cigars and rationed them carefully. They were all gone now and he was frantic for a smoke. Joe rolled his own cigarettes, didn't have extra tobacco, and refused to share.

One night the Northern Lights lit up the northern sky. Stars glittered overhead in the clear air. Skim ice had formed around the lake shore by dawn. The following day the dwarf arctic birch, quaking aspen and bearberries were vibrant yellows, browns and reds. Joe couldn't believe that autumn had arrived so swiftly. Then he remembered how sometimes, at home in Ketchikan, even with warm balmy weather at sea level, they'd wake one fall morning and see Deer Mountain dusted with snow. And they were higher here than the top of Deer Mountain, in the bitter cold interior and a lot closer to the cold Coast Range.

Remembering how Scotty and his partner had been caught in a snow storm, got lost because they didn't have a compass, and nearly froze to death, Joe decided to leave, with or without Hugo. Both men were slowly going crazy with boredom, and Joe was concerned about his wife. He had kept their plans so quiet, that no one, except the pilot, had the slightest idea of where they were! Not that this was important. Even if they'd told someone, no one could have came looking for them without another aircraft anyway. Now even Joe admitted to himself they'd been insane to fly in here.

Joe set a date. At the end of the third week they were leaving. They would leave a note, in case the pilot returned, so that at least he knew what happened.

The following day the north wind picked up and it began to snow. Thoroughly frightened, Joe told Hugo that he was leaving, with or without him, as soon as the snow and wind quit. For three days a cold north wind blew and two feet of snow fell. They split the heavy canvas army tent, took half for a lean-to shelter, which still weighed 10 pounds, left the useless shot gun and a message in a can hanging on a stick by the landing place, and headed west. Joe hoped they could reach Telegraph Creek in a week.

He misjudged the distance, the terrain and Hugo's traveling ability. Hugo's slick-shod shoes were not made for steep country, where Joe's boots were equipped with hob nails. Joe wrapped Hugo's boot soles with fish twine, which helped, but soon wore out. He fell often, cursing Joe for getting him into such a situation.

Sitting around camp for six weeks had allowed Hugo to become soft, while Joe was used to walking with a pack. Hugo complained his pack was too heavy. He threw away several items without Joe's noticing.

By mid-day, Hugo would become so weary he wanted to camp for the night. It took all of Joe's resolve not to simply walk away and leave him. He pleaded and begged Hugo to keep going. When they finally did stop for the night, Hugo plopped down and refused to help with camp chores.

Remembering Scotty's warning about following the wrong watershed, Joe held to a compass course towards the Tuya River, but the lay of the land kept throwing him off. Looking down from the airplane one didn't notice when crossing from one watershed to another on the mostly level plateau. Now he understood how Scotty and Cass, under cloudy skies and without a compass, had easily became confused and descended into the wrong watershed, thinking they were descending into the headwaters of the Tuya. Without the compass he would have made the same mistake.

Joe had trouble maintaining his course, and it involved much climbing and descending. Dropping into a snow-free valley far below was tempting. Snow fell intermittently higher up.

Hugo, sliding and slipping on the steep ground, fell frequently and kept urging Joe to head down hill, to get below the snow. Joe said he had the compass, knew where they had to go, and dropping into the valley would only lead them astray. They needed to hold their elevation until they found the headwaters of the Tuya.

Hugo was angry and scared. He often sat down in the snow, begging Joe for tobacco, and talked about giving up, claiming they had been traveling for four days and hadn't even began to cover any distance.

Joe couldn't take any more of this. "That's your fault. Okay, stay here then." Joe turned his back and started off. He'd absolutely had it with Hugo's attitude. Several times he was tempted to turn back, because leaving Hugo behind amounted to certain death. Joe was carrying the compass, tarp and rifle. But sticking with him was almost certain death too, because Hugo traveled so slowly.

Before dark, Joe set up camp and built a fire to melt snow. At dark he fired the rifle to let Hugo know where he was.

Shortly after dark Hugo stumbled into camp and plopped down by the fire. "Thought you'd got rid of me, didn't you Joe?"

"Well, I'm glad you decided to catch up. You know it would be in both of our interests to try and get along." From then on, Hugo was a different person. They even began talking to each other again. Hugo tried harder to keep up.

Joe thought he was passing through the area where Scotty and Cass had cached the picture rock, part of the nuggets and extra camp equipment after they lost the mule. He kept a sharp eye out for the rock slide and big rock. Several times he discovered rock slides that fit the description, and wasted a lot of time and energy digging through the snow and removing rocks from around large boulders without results.

Hugo used this time to rest, calling Joe a fool, that there was no cache of gold.

Day after day they backpacked through rough country, sometimes having to detour around impassible mountainsides, lakes and yawning ravines. They saw little game.

Caribou jerky, oatmeal and rice was their fare. Bacon, tobacco, sugar, flour, dried fruit were all gone. Hugo had used up their coffee supply before they started walking out.

At night, huddled over a fire trying to dry their clothes and shoes, they began thinking up hideous schemes to torture, even kill the pilot once they caught up with him.

One plan was to kidnap him, haul him and a few basic supplies out to some tiny, remote, rocky islet in Joe's boat, then set him free and abandon him for the same period of time they had been abandoned.

Hugo decided they should destroy Crazy Charlie's plane so he couldn't carry others into the wilderness and abandon them. It was harmless amusement, and kept their spirits up. Joe remembered some of the torture techniques were pretty gruesome.

Finally, in the Tuya River Valley, they ate the last of their food. Backpacking is strenuous work. Within two days they were both so weak they could barely keep going. They had only three cartridges for the rifle left.

At night, Joe used strong fish twine to set snares in rabbit trails. All they caught was a marten. They skinned and roasted the pitiful little creature. The meat made Joe sick at his stomach. Hugo refused to touch it.

They came across a porcupine, killed it with a club, built a fire, roasted, then devoured the little animal on the spot.

One day, after they'd became so weak they could hardly walk, Joe spotted a young moose browsing willows in a thicket. Using all his stalking ability, saying a silent prayer, he crawled down wind through the snow, tall grass and willows, crept to within a few yards and shot the moose in the head, killing it instantly.

Without the moose, Joe believes they would have both died, because they didn't see another moose or caribou. They camped for two days, feasting on the fat and meat, jerking and smoking some of the meat, although their salt supply was gone.

About one month after leaving the lake they reached Telegraph Creek. They were both skin and bones and their clothing hung on them like sacks. They walked into Frank Calbreath's log trading post and caused quite a stir. Their boots mere scraps of leather, bound with moose hide.

Frank Calbreath had taken over his father's store in 1910 after John retired, and had seen some mighty rough-looking men come by, but Joe and Hugo were as tough looking as they came.

"When is the last boat to Wrangell?" they asked.

"Two weeks ago."

"There's no more?"

"Not until breakup next spring."

"How do we get out of here?"

Calbreath took his time loading his pipe and lighting it. "Well, you can walk. It's only 1,500 miles to Vancouver."

Both men sank down on a bench inside the store in despair.. "Can we get something to eat? And some tobacco," Hugo asked.

Callbreath spoke to an Indian woman. She disappeared to the back of the store. She soon motioned for them to come to the kitchen, where she served them heaping plates of cornbread and bowls of stew. They noticed she didn't linger nearby. It suddenly occurred to them that it had been two months since they'd had a bath.

After they'd eaten their fill they returned to the store.

Calbreath was writing in his ledger. "I have an empty cabin. Last one up the hill. Why don't you go up there, build a fire, heat some water and take a bath. There's a tin tub hanging on the back of the store."

"Can we get credit to buy some new cloths?" Hugo asked.

"I suppose so." Calbreath gave them each a pair of socks, long underwear, overalls, boots and a shirt, entering each item in his ledger.

Calbreath's store at Telegraph Creek, probably late 1890s.

The small log cabin contained a double bed, wood stove with a flat top for cooking and several wooden boxes nailed to the walls for storage. They built a fire and heated buckets of water. After a bath and new clothes, they felt like humans again. They spread their sleeping bags on the bed and were soon snoring.

Dawn was breaking when Calbreath came in with an armload of kindling. "You fellows slept all night, huh. Pretty tired, I'll bet." He built a fire.

"Come on down for breakfast when you're ready," Calbreath said.

"He seems like a nice guy. Do you think he'll let us use one of his river skiffs?" Hugo said.

"We can ask."

After they finished a breakfast of sourdough pancakes and coffee, Joe asked if they could rent or borrow a skiff. The trader refused, saying the slower, lower river froze long before the swift upper, and they might become trapped in the ice. If they did, death was inevitable.

"What are we to do then?

"See that big pile of logs by the boat landing. They all have to be bucked into stove wood. I'll provide a cabin, flour, beans and bacon. You cut wood, daylight until dark, six days a week. Sundays you can hunt your own meat."

"That's a lot of wood," Joe said.

"You have any idea how much wood it takes to keep this store warm during eight months of below freezing weather? A lot. I also sell wood to my renters. Soon as that pile has been cut into stove-sized lengths, you can take the horses and sled, go out along the river and start cutting next year's supply."

They were presented with saws, an axe and splitting maul. During the next week they faithfully cut wood. Calbreath provided them the basic foods, a few pots and pans and several blankets. He wrote it all down in his ledger.

On Sunday Joe left at daylight to hunt. Although he walked all day, he came in after dark empty handed. "There's no game around here. It's been hunted out by the local Indians. What are we going to do for meat?" he growled.

"Sowbelly. Putrid, moldy sowbelly," Hugo spat.

Darkness came at five o'clock. They had a coal oil lantern for light in the cabin, and plenty of books from a library in the store. The nights were unbearably long.

One day Joe flung down the saw and rolled a cigarette. "I don't know about you, Hugo, but I'd just as soon take my chances on the river as living on beans and looking across a frozen log at your ugly face for seven months."

For once, Hugo agreed. They secretly began gathering what they needed, a little food, their Hudson Bay blankets, tobacco, shells for the rifle, and hiding it under the bed where the trader

131

wouldn't see it while prowling around the cabin while they were sawing wood.

Each Saturday night the local people, mostly Indians, got together in the trading post and danced to music from a record player. The first Saturday, Joe and Hugo attended. They were surprised that Calbreath sold the Indians liquor, and drank plenty himself. When he was asked about it, he smiled and said, "Aw, the Queen is far away." By midnight most of the dancers were drunk and whooping it up.

The following Saturday, they attended the dance again. About two in the morning the party broke up. A light snow was falling as they went up the hill to the cabin. As soon as it was quiet, they left a note saying they would pay for the gear they'd bought and the boat as soon as they could or leave the boat in Wrangell to be towed back to Telegraph Creek in the spring. Shortly before daylight they carried their camping equipment to the boat landing. Two 24-foot river boats were drawn up on the bank. They found two sets of oars, shoved one into the current and were off.

For a while everything went well. They stopped and built a fire at night, tipped the boat up on edge as a shelter, wrapped in their blankets before the fire and slept soundly. Late one afternoon they drifted into what they later learned was Whirlpool Canyon. The river flowed straight against a sheer rock cliff, then circled around, causing a gigantic whirlpool. The heavy, clumsy boat began circling round and round. Each time they came near the tail race, they rowed as hard as they could, but the current was so strong they found themselves circling again. Darkness set in by five o'clock. Round and round they went, the roar of the river beneath their boat was frightening, especially after dark.

When questioned by this writer later, this incident in Whirlpool Canyon was reported differently by each man. Joe claimed that Hugo decided they were goners, and would simply die from exposure in the whirlpool. He told Joe he was ending his misery by jumping overboard. Joe grabbed hold of Hugo. They fell onto the floorboards, flailing at each other with their fists in the dark. Finally they lay back on the floorboards exhausted.

Hugo laughed hysterically.

"What's funny?"

"This's the first time I've been warm since we left Telegraph Creek," Hugo said.

I worked for Hugo Schmolck for several years at Schmolck's Plumbing and Heating on the Alaska Steamship Company dock. He was a fine man, and a good boss. During all the time I worked for him, we never had a problem. He was reluctant to talk about his adventure with Joe into the Canadian wilderness. When I pressing him for details, he only shrugged and said, "That happened back when I was young and foolish." I questioned him about exactly happened that night in Whirlpool Canyon, mentioning that Joe claimed it was Hugo that tried to end it all by jumping overboard. Hugo bristled. The old hatred flared up. "It was the other way around. It was Joe who wanted to jump overboard and end it all," he spat. "It was me that held onto him and beat some sense into his stupid head."

The night in Whirlpool Canyon would have been a nightmare for anyone. As the night wore on, a stiff, icy wind blew down the river. The boat circled around and around the whirlpool, black cliffs looming overhead, then the noise of gravel rolling as they neared the tail race, at which signal they would row desperately, trying to break free.

Finally, too tired to keep on rowing, they huddled beneath their blankets, their feet freezing, and suffered the cold wind and snow, waiting for whatever fate decided. Sometime during the pitch dark night they noticed they were no longer circling, but were drifting down the river. The fickle current had accomplished what they could not and mysteriously ejected them from the whirlpool.

In total darkness they faced another even greater danger. The Stikine is notorious for its many "sweepers." Large spruce and cottonwood trees, undermined by the current, that have fallen into the river. Many had limbs sticking down into the water, creating dangerous "strainers." If a boat was caught on the up-current side of a sweeper, the craft would be rolled underwater. There would be no escape.

They rowed ashore, landed on a rocky ledge devoid of firewood and spent the rest of the night kicking their cold feet against the side of the boat.

At daylight they noticed a large Sitka spruce tree that had fallen into the river a short ways below where they had spent the night. The trunk protruded out from the bank, level with the water. Limbs stuck down into the river.

"That was too close for comfort," Joe said.

They were lucky. They encountered only a few patches of skim ice during the 160 miles to the river mouth.

At the Customs House near the border, they stopped and spent the night. The building was abandoned. They built a roaring fire in the huge barrel stove and slept warm for a change.

As they entered the tidal area near the mouth, a winter gale was blowing. The shallow mouth of the Stikine is a dangerous place. When the river current meets the swells a wide band of dangerous breakers occur. They went down Knik Slough and took refuge from the storm in the protection of the spruce forest on Farm Island. There was plenty of drift wood, and they kept a fire going. They had 10 shells left. Joe shot a deer. They couldn't get enough of the fat meat.

Cold rain poured down night and day. A week went by before the storm let up. By then their venison was gone. One morning at high water they pushed off and rode the last of the ebb down Knik Slough and across the bar. Before they reached Wrangell, only six miles away, a southeast wind sprang up again and it took them all day to row to town. Both were so weak and tired they could hardly walk to a nearby restaurant for a good meal. The waitress looked at them curiously. They overheard her telling the cook, "Those two have been well smoked."

Next they went to the bar where they'd stopped on their way upriver.

The bartender didn't recognize them. After they announced who they were, the bartender poured them a drink on the house, and admitted he was surprised to see them.

"When you didn't show up on the last boat, everyone assumed you two were dead," he said.

"Why would you think that?" Joe asked. "Why wouldn't you assume our pilot flew in and picked us up?"

"You don't know, then?"

"Know what? We don't know anything. We just walked out of the Cassiar and floated down the river."

The bartender pursed his lips thoughtfully, and poured them another drink on the house. "My God. You walked out! How did you get down the river?"

"In a skiff. Did that damn pilot show up in Wrangell? Or did he crash on the way out?"

"He showed up, but a day later. Claimed he got lost in some clouds and had to land on the river. Nearly ran out of gas. That was two months ago."

"Well, as you can see, he never came back to get us. We've got a score to settle with him. Did he say anything when he stopped here?"

"Did some drinking, and a lot of talking about how he was soon going to be rich." The bartender took a long look at both men. "You two don't look very rich to me."

"We're anything but rich."

"Anyway, if you two are looking for that pilot, what was his name, Charlie? I'm afraid you're outta luck. Week or so after he returned to Ketchikan, he took a passenger and departed for Seattle. Claimed he had a big mining contract coming up and needed something with more power. Ain't been seen nor heard of since. The customs people checked at Alert Bay, where he would have had to stop for gas. He never got that far. Never showed up at Lake Union either. Say, I'll bet your wives are worried about you."

Hugo and Joe looked at each other. Hugo was the first to speak. "I hope there's a mail boat we can ride to Ketchikan on. I'm not flying in no damn plane."

"There's no plane anywhere in Southeast Alaska. The mail-boat leaves in two days."

True to his word, Hugo disliked planes the rest of his life. When he and his wife went south on a trip, they usually traveled from Ketchikan to Vancouver, or Seattle on either Alaska Steamship Company ships, or the Canadian Princess Lines.

Epilogue

As soon as Joe and Hugo arrived back in Ketchikan they sent a telegram to Telegraph Creek explaining they had arrived at Wrangell safely, had made arrangements for the river skiff to be stored for the winter and towed back to Telegraph Creek in the spring, and would send money to pay their bill at the trading post as soon as they could. Otherwise they knew Calbreath would put out a warrant for their arrest.

Although both Joe and Hugo lived in Ketchikan for decades, the two men never spoke. They refused to serve on the same committees, or attend the same functions. They hated each other's guts to the end.

Joe Krause eventually bought the *FV Tyee* and seined salmon for New England Fish Company.

Years later, during the early 1950s, living on Peterson Avenue next door to Joe, I used to spend winter evenings visiting in his workshop. I was new to the North in those days and eagerly sought any lore about boating, mining and gold. I took an extension course on mining from the University of Alaska School of Mines, and prospected when I found time.

Joe was impressed because of my taking the course and by my keen interest in Alaska. We spent a lot of time pouring over charts of Southeast Alaska, with Joe pointing out areas of interest.

One night I told him how I'd just came from a grocery store where Oscar Newlund had shown me a quart fruit jar full of rough gold he'd found on Prince of Wales Island. I was excited to think gold was still available for those who looked for it..

Joe scoffed. "That's nothing. I know where there's a placer mine so rich you can pick up a fortune with your fingers."

"Tell me about it?" I thought he was kidding.

Then he clammed up. I forgot about his boast, although Joe wasn't the type to boast. A few days later he motioned me into his workshop, and began telling me, little by little, about looking for the mine with my boss, Hugo Schmolck, and how they'd nearly died walking out after being abandoned by an airline pilot in the wilds of British Columbia.

This was fascinating stuff for a young man interested in mining. I hung onto every word, wondering if it was true or not. As the story unfolded, Joe warmed to the idea of telling me about his experiences on the wild Stikine Plateau. One night, with a southeast gale beating rain against the sides of the work-shop, Joe pulled out a worn notebook and fragile, aged map. Swearing me to secrecy, Joe showed me his treasures.

After going home, I made a rough sketch of Joe's detailed map and wrote a few notes of my own. In 1954 we bought a home at Mile 6½ Mountain Point. I hid the notes and map in the upstairs rafters. Did I ever think about the mine? Many times. Did I ever consider trying to locate it? Yes. But like Joe, I had a family to think about, and lived from payday to payday working for Schmolck Plumbing and Heating in town. Then we rented the house and moved to Sitka while I worked building the Sitka Pulp Mill at Silver Bay. By the time we moved back to Ketchikan in 1959, I had bought a 43-foot salmon troller, the *Laverne II*, and that kept me occupied.

During the winter, while the rain poured down and the south-east winds blew, I sometimes found Joe hanging out in the galley of the *Tyee* at her berth in Thomas Basin. We'd drink coffee and complain about the weather, but the talk, if no one else was present, usually got around to mining, and the Fishhook Lake Mine.

Joe had no intentions of looking for it again. One experience in the Cassiar wilderness was enough. He always remained close mouthed about it and I think he was sorry he ever told me the story in the first place. Since he liked me, I may be the only one he ever told. Until now, I've honored his wish of secrecy.

Eventually my wife and I split up and I moved south, forgetting the map. She sold the house. It later burned to the ground, destroying my copy of the map.

South of Ketchikan, at the entrance to Ham Island Pass, is a submerged rock, locally known as Joe Krause Rock, perhaps the only feature in his beloved Southeast Alaska named for Joe Krause. Had things been different, a rich mine could have carried his name.

One day Joe was at the helm of the *Tyee*, headed into the Pass. He pointed off to one side and told the crewman standing at his elbow, "There's a sunken rock right over there." Just then the *Tyee* struck the rock. They got the boat into the Pass, beached it on the nice sand beach there, cut up several pairs of hip boots to place a patch on the forefoot and ran her to the shipyard in Ketchikan for repairs.

Has the writer ever consider looking for the mine?

Sure, lots of times. But every time I thought about trying to find the mine, I remembered the suffering four men had experienced, and chickened out.

Do I know about where the Fishhook Lake Mine is? If I knew, I'd go and stake it. My best guess, after extensive research and study of new maps of the area, would be in the vicinity of Meta Mountain, elevation 5,960 feet, which itself lies in a confusing area, on the divide between Kahn Creek, that drains into the Jennings River and Krdahda River, a tributary of the Teslin River. This is a vast expanse of wild country lying some 80 miles as the raven flies south of Milepost 719 on the Alaska Highway. Recent maps show some trails through this area, and hundreds of lakes.

I have one other valid reason to believe this is a likely area, because Guy Lawrence, mentioned in connection with the Yukon Telegraph Company, who served a total of 40 years in the Telegraph Service in Northern British Columbia, discovered a rich gold vein in the area. Lawrence was transferred to Nahlin in 1904. Nahlin Station was 97 miles north of Telegraph Creek and 130 miles south of Atlin.

In 1930, while serving at Stewart, W.B. George, a mining man, noticed the rich chunk of float ore lying on Lawrence's desk and asked where it had came from. Lawrence told him he had found it while hunting sheep on a high pass some 14 miles north of Nahlin Station in 1904 while an operator there. Since Lawrence had leave coming in May, the two men decided to return to the area. They went up the Stikine River on one of Barrington Brothers diesel-powered boats to Telegraph Creek and walked the old abandoned trail to Nahlin, then to the mountain. Unfortunately, a late spring had left deep snow covering the area where he'd found the float.

Again, in 1946, with a mining engineer, Lawrence visited the area, flying from Vancouver to Carcross, then changing to a small amphibious plane for the flight to a lake near the location. This time they were also disappointed. During the last 16 years a massive, 60-foot-deep rock slide had covered the area where he had found the float.

Joe died in Oregon March 6, 1970. His wife, Florence, died several years later, also in Oregon. They had no children.

Hugo Schmolck married Gladys, a wonderful lady, who did book keeping for Schmolck Plumbing and Heating. And, in his younger days, he didn't have such an aversion to the outdoors as Joe implied. He was a member of the Alaska Sportsmen's Association in 1937, and active in transplanting elk to the Ward Lake area, and Chinese pheasants to other parts of the island. Neither transplants were successful. Hugo and Gladys were beloved citizens of Ketchikan. At retirement, they sold the business to William Goodale, now of Sequim, Washington, retired and moved to Woodburn, Oregon, where Hugo died.

Schmolck Plumbing still exists in Ketchikan and is owned by Bill Goodale Jr.

Why did it take me all these years to write this story? Several reasons. I actually wrote most of it many years ago, but like Joe Krause, had other things to do. I'd hoped to locate the name of the pilot and what kind of plane he had. By the time I realized I needed the pilot's name to complete the story, Joe and Hugo were both dead. Although I've exhausted every source I can think of, I've never learned who he was or what kind of plane it was that flew Joe and Hugo into the wilds. If you look at the enclosed photograph of the Vickers Viking at Dease Lake in 1925, (page 117) you'll have a good idea of what the plane may have looked like.

While I lived at Mountain Point, several neighbors were pilots. One, Don Ross, had distinguished himself by finding the first uranium deposit in Alaska on Bokan Mountain, Prince of Wales Island. He and his wife, Jan, made this find while flying with a scintillation counter attached to his aircraft, an instrument that registers radiation. For being the first to locate uranium in a new region, they received quite a nice reward from the government.

Don had also flown extensively in British Columbia on prospecting trips, sometimes with his partner, Kelly Adams. They had some hair-raising and interesting experiences, but that's another story. When I discretely asked Don if he'd ever flown the Stikine Plateau, and what it was like, he said he'd flown over part of it. "Big, wild, high, remote country," he said. "No place to blow a piston rod."

Forty years ago, a couple local pilots thought it was cool to fly into British Columbia in their private planes, without notifying authorities, or buying a licence, and bag a moose. "Queen's Beef" they called it. One, who's name I'll not mention, although he is no longer alive, and was a respected citizen of Ketchikan, had landed on a lake in the Tuya Lake area and shot a moose. He described the area as a paradise, beautiful, waist-high grass, rolling hills, patches of birch and quaking aspen, and lots of fat game animals, but some rugged mountains nearby.

At Dease Lake, British Columbia, my son Robert and I stopped at the Department of Energy, Mines and Resources to buy maps of the Stikine Plateau. The man who supplied them inquired why we wanted maps of that area.

"I'm looking for a lost mine," I said.

141

"Ah, one of those," he said. There was no mistaking his interest. "Is there placer gold up there?"

"Is there wheat in Alberta?" He showed us a nice nugget on a chain around his neck. "That's where this came from," he said.

This area is heavily mineralized. Several gold mines are still operating in the Cassiar. One of the world's largest suppliers of chrysotile asbestos was discovered at Cassiar, Milepost 372.5 northbound on the Cassiar Highway. Local Indians called the area "snowball mountain" because of outcroppings of white, fluffy mineral, frayed by the wind. The mine closed in 1992 and we were stopped from visiting by a locked gate in 1996. Cassiar is not far east, as the crow flies, from the reported location of the Fishhook Lake Mine.

While attending the United States/Canada Salmon Discussions, as an Industry Representative for the U.S. Department of State, in Vancouver, British Columbia, in 1968, I listened with great interest while a Canadian fisheries biologist described the salmon rearing potential of the upper Tuya River watershed. At the time the United States and Canada were discussing joint enhancement projects that might increase salmon production for both nations. A falls near the river's confluence with the Stikine prevented salmon from going up the Tuya River.

After the session, I questioned him about the country. He's the only person, beside Joe and Hugo, I've ever spoken with who has actually walked part of the Tuya River Valley. I asked him what the area was like. He described the upper river as a beautiful salmon habitat, with many spawning areas. The lower river was rough and rugged, with canyons and cliffs, and of course a falls that prevented salmon from ascending. I asked him what it would be like to backpack a heavy load, say 60 pounds, down out of the mountains to the east and north of Tuya Lake to Telegraph Creek, during winter conditions?

Surprised by the question, he said, "I doubt if anyone would ever do that."

I didn't tell him at least four men had.

This same area also produces high-quality jade, and Jade City, Milepost 371.3 on the Cassiar Highway, bills itself as the "jade capitol" of the world.

I asked Jim Ruotsala, of Juneau, Alaska, who is dedicated to Alaska's aviation history, and author of *Pilots of the Panhandle*, if he knew who the pilot that flew Joe and Hugo into the Cassiar could have been. He didn't.

When I inquired if he thought it was possible that a pilot and plane could have been operating in Southeast Alaska during the early 1930s without leaving a record, he admitted it was unlikely, but certainly possible, since there were no regulations about such things.

Is the gold still there? The cache at Dead Mule certainly is, but how many hundred rock slides are in the area? Who knows if the rock slide remains the same as it did over a century ago?

What happened to Cass's share of the gold? The Tahltans didn't set much value in gold, but they certainly would have known how to spend it. There was no indication that Charlie suddenly became rich and squandered gold at Telegraph Creek. Perhaps they recovered the gold and simply never admitted it.

If the sled carrying Cass went through the ice, it seems doubtful that all the dogs and others in the party would have gone down also, but one never knows.

Since the use of aircraft, especially helicopters, there is no unexplored wilderness left in the North, at least unexplored from the air. A great deal of mining has been done throughout the Stikine Plateau region.

Remember, the mine was reportedly in a location that is only snow free a short period of the summer, and it's a hillside placer, with no stream nearby. Consequently, who would be looking for placer gold in such a place?

Suggested Reading and Bibliography

Adney, Tappan, THE KLONDIKE STAMPEDE (Harpers & Brothers,1900, second edition, 1994 UBC Press) Mr. Adney was a reporter for *Harpers Weekly* and the *London Chronicle*. He sailed from Victoria on August 15, 1897 on the *Islander*, went over Chilkoot Pass, drifted down the Yukon to Dawson, built a log cabin on Bonanza Creek, then spent 16 months documenting the Klondike area. His detailed acounts are this writer's favorite source for the greatest gold rush in North America.

Afflek, Edward L., THE SEA CHEST, Journal of the Puget Sound Maritime Historical Society, Pgs 37-48 (Seattle, Sept. 1998)

Mitcham, Allison, TAKU, the heart of North America's last great wilderness (Lancelot Press, Hantsport, Nova Scotia, 1993)

Lawrence, Guy, "The Stikine Trail," BRITISH COLUMBIA DIGEST (Vol. 20, No 6, Nov.-Dec., 1964)

Hacking, Norman. CAPTAIN WILLIAM MOORE—B.C'S AMAZING FRONTIERSMAN (Heritage House, 1993)

THE STIKINE RIVER, Alaska Geographic (Vol. 6, No. 4, 1979)

DOGS OF THE NORTH, Alaska Geographic (Vol.14, No 1, 1987)

Lawrence, Guy, 40 YEARS ON THE YUKON TELEGRAPH (Reprinted, Caryall Books, Quesnel, B.C, 1990)

Ruotsala, Jim, PILOTS OF THE PANHANDLE (Seadrome Press, Juneau, 1997)

Dickenson & Smith, Christine Frances and Diane Solie,
ATLIN, the story of British Columbia's last gold rush (Atlin
Historical Society, Atlin, B.C, 1995)

James A. Johnson, CARMACKS OF THE KLONDIKE
(Epicenter Press, 1990)

Hacking, Norman, marine historian and newspaper columnist
of Victoria. I borrowed heavily from Mr. Hacking's five-part
series in B.C. OUTDOORS, for the information about
Captain William Moore and his family, gleaned, I under
stand, from valuable family letters and documents.

About The Author

Author/Photographer Francis E. Caldwell has published four previous books, Pacific Troller, The Ebb and the Flood, Land of the Ocean Mists, Beyond the Trails, and hundreds of magazine articles, mostly about travel, photography, outdoor and adventure subjects.

He moved to Alaska in 1950 where he worked in construction and salmon fishing. In 1958 he began commercial fishing full time and spent forty years as a fishing vessel owner. Retiring from fishing in 1995, he began photographing and writing full-time.

He travels extensively, to Alaska, Africa, Asia, Western Canada, South and Central America, the West Indies and Mexico to photograph and gather material for travel articles and slide shows.

He and his wife Donna operate AFFORDABLE PHOTO STOCK, a library containing 100,000 photos of wildlife, nature, travel, people and documentary subjects. Their photos have been published throughout the world in magazines and books. In 1998 they formed ANCHOR PUBLISHING and published their first title, Beyond the Trails, about Olympic National Park.

Caldwell is a member of the Outdoor Writers Association of America, American Society of Media Photographers, Northwest Outdoor Writers Association and North American Nature Photographers.

When not traveling, the Caldwells reside in Port Angeles, Washington. Favorite activities are backpacking, kayaking, photographing and RVing. Their email address is dlc@olypen.com. To visit their web site:www.agpix.com/affordablephoto

ISBN 155212337-5

9 781552 123379